Robyn Hood

Robyn Hood

Outlaw Princess

JOHN REYNOLDS

Starblaze Publications
Auckland, New Zealand

Published by Starblaze Publications

Starblaze Publications
10A Law Street, Torbay 0630, Auckland, New Zealand
Email: jbess@vodafone.co.nz

www. drjohnreynolds.com

A catalogue record for this book is available from the National Library of New Zealand.

Juvenile fiction, legends, time travel

Cover photo: John Reynolds
Cover design: AnitaTaylorDesign.com
Model: Victoria Hutt

To Emilia and Olivia

May you both realise your dreams

Contents

Chapter 1

"What are you girls doing?" The school principal was striding towards them.

"Smelly. Just our luck," whispered Janice.

Reaching the group he hunched his shoulders and glowered at each of the four in turn.

"Well?" he demanded.

"Er, hello, Mr Smallfield. We're just on our way to History class," said Sophie, striving to adopt an innocent expression.

"History." His glare increased.

"Yes, History, Mr Smallfield. That's what she said."

The principal stared balefully at the tall girl at the back of the group. "Robyn Howard, isn't it?"

"Yes."

"Yes, what?"

"Yes, that's my name."

The other three girls hurriedly stepped aside as the principal advanced towards Robyn.

"Robyn Howard. Of course. I've been hearing reports about you. Not only are you a distraction in class, you're also frequently late. The fact that you're still here would seem to provide confirmation."

"That's not fair. We've only just finished soccer practice. I'm the captain and it's my responsibility–"

"Your responsibility, Robyn Howard, is to get to class on time. And to pay attention to what the teacher is saying."

"But Mr Smallfield," said Robyn, "all we ever do is listen and write things down. If I try to ask a question or offer an opinion, I'm told to stop talking and get on with my work. It's so boring!"

"Seems to me, young lady, that being captain of the soccer team has gone to your head."

"That's not fair–"

"Silence, girl! You are rude, and insolent." The principal leaned forward, his face so close she could see the hairs in his left nostril moving as he breathed heavily. "And you are late for your History class."

Robyn flinched but stood her ground, meeting his angry stare.

"You other girls, go!" he snapped.

As they hurried away he turned back to Robyn.

"Now, Robyn Howard. As punishment for your insolence you will attend after-school detention." He smiled malevolently. "Today!"

"Today? But–"

"You will write me a five hundred-word essay on the lives of three famous men in history."

"Today. Five hundred words."

In spite of herself, Robyn took a step back. Smallfield followed, his face still uncomfortably close to hers.

"Do you understand?"

"Yes."

"Yes, what?"

"Yes, I understand."

"Do you want me to increase–"

"Yes, I understand, Mr Smallfield."

"Excellent. You and your laptop will be busy this afternoon."

"I suppose so."

"Do you–"

"Yes, Mr Smallfield."

Stepping back, he regarded her for a moment and then with a smirk said, "Hurry along to your History class, girl. You're already far too late."

Chapter 2

Robyn's footsteps echoed in the long empty corridor as she walked slowly towards the classroom at the far end. From either side came the sounds of teachers' voices mixed with their students' responses.

Eastlake College had more than a thousand students, both girls and boys, the photos on the corridor walls displaying evidence of its high sporting and academic reputation.

But Robyn wasn't in the mood to consider the school in a positive light. She was burning with resentment at the principal's treatment of her, and the tedious prospect of an afternoon detention. Reaching the classroom door at the end of the corridor she paused, took a deep breath, opened it and stepped inside.

"Sorry, Miss Robinson."

"Ah, Robyn."

"I had to talk to the principal."

"Indeed." Miss Robinson smiled. She was one of the youngest teachers on the staff and was very popular with the students. "No problems, I hope?"

Robyn hesitated. Although still angry after her confrontation, she liked Miss Robinson. "No, Miss Robinson."

"Glad to hear it. You're a bright girl, Robyn, but at times you do tend a little towards verbosity."

"Verb– what?"

"You talk too much, a common problem with girls of your age. Now, take your seat."

As she passed Sophie, Robyn paused and murmured, "Thanks for leaving me to face him."

"Robyn! Verbosity!"

"Sorry, Miss Robinson."

Robyn quickly seated herself and looked up at her teacher.

"Now, girls, as I was saying, King Henry the Eighth had six wives."

"Six wives?" called Robyn. "Were the women all mad?"

"No, Robyn. It was mostly to do with politics."

"It generally is with men in history. If women had been running countries back then, it would have been different."

"History *is* mostly about men I'm afraid, Robyn. They were in charge. They were the kings, princes, nobles, barons, and knights. Women played a secondary role."

"Well, it shouldn't have been that way."

"But it was. Although times have changed to some extent, back then important events were very largely determined by men."

Robyn shrugged. "Suppose so. Wish I'd lived back then. I'd have shown them."

"I daresay, Robyn," said her teacher, smiling.

The rest of the lesson was quite interesting, but Robyn was distracted by her sense of injustice. Five hundred words would not be a problem, although she certainly had better things to do with her time. Smelly had singled her out because she always spoke her mind. He seemed to relish confrontation because it gave him the opportunity to show his authority. "Huh. The lives of three famous men in history," she muttered.

"What was that, Robyn?"

Startled from her thoughts, Robyn looked up at the teacher.

"Oh, nothing, Miss Robinson. Just thinking aloud."

"Verbosity even in your dreams, Robyn. Please try to concentrate."

"Yes, miss."

No point in falling out with two staff members in one afternoon.

Like Miss Robinson, most of the teachers at Eastlake High School were okay. Yet at seventeen, Robyn was feeling increasingly irritated by the number of rules and restrictions. She did well in her subjects, was captain of the soccer eleven and was popular with the other girls. Yet she always felt constricted by the school environment, by always being told what to do by other people. Maybe in a different place, in a different time... She caught Miss Robinson's frown and quickly straightened herself up with an innocent smile, just as the bell signalled the end of the school day.

Chapter 3

Robyn quickly left the classroom. The day had started badly, and detention was the last thing she needed. Wanting to be by herself, she headed towards the corner of the deserted soccer field and, with a long sigh, sat down under a tall tree.

That morning she'd come down to breakfast expecting to chat with her mother about their weekend plans. They rarely spent time together, as her mum's job often took her away from home. Although Robyn enjoyed time by herself or with friends, she still valued her mum's company. She looked up to her as a successful person with a prestigious career in the fashion industry – but she couldn't help resenting the frequent absences. Her friends often had both parents attending school functions, while Robyn's dad generally came alone.

Dad was an amiable man and, in contrast to Robyn's mum, was quiet and rather shy. Although at times she wished he could be more assertive, his gentle nature had created a warm father-daughter relationship. Her earliest memories were filled with Dad taking her to the beach, looking after her childhood injuries, reading her stories at night and helping her with homework. He'd come to all her school plays, prize-givings and sports matches, occasionally accompanied by her mother.

It was Dad who'd given Robyn an interest in history. For as long as she could remember, he'd read her stories about people from other times and places, her favourites being tales of knights and ladies of medieval times. As she'd grown older, she'd questioned him as to why the knights seemed to have all the excitement and adventures, while the women stayed at home. Her father had no answer, other than to say that was how things were in those days.

Over the past two years he'd developed an enthusiasm for genealogy, and had begun tracing the Howard family's English ancestry. He told her that the name Howard originated from the Anglo Saxon tribes that once ruled England.

"They lived in the east of England, in an area between Norwich and Nottingham," he'd explained. "Some of them fought in King Richard's army."

"The one called Richard the Lionheart?" asked Robyn.

"Yes, that's him. It also seems that some members of the family in the town of Nottingham were declared outlaws."

"Like Robin Hood of Sherwood Forest. That's near Nottingham, isn't it?"

"Yes it is. Some outlaws like Robin Hood were regarded as heroes, particularly if the ruler was cruel. Others were seen as criminals."

"By the rulers."

"Exactly."

"So we had outlaws in our family?"

"Yes." Her dad grinned. "It's probably where you inherited your rebellious nature."

Robyn smiled to herself as she recalled his words. Then the smile faded as she remembered their conversation at breakfast this morning.

"Fresh from the toaster, Robyn," Dad had said, putting a rack of toast in front of her. "Golden brown. Just how you like it."

She'd frowned at the false enthusiasm of his voice.

"It's only toast, Dad."

He'd turned away quickly and reached for the morning paper.

Robyn had looked around. "Where's Mum?"

"Mum?"

"Yes, Dad. She said she'd see me at breakfast and we could talk about Sunday's archery practice."

The night before, at a rare family evening meal, Robyn's mum had suggested she and Robyn spend Sunday afternoon at the archery club. Although soccer was Robyn's favourite sport, she was beginning to do well in archery – a sport that had always been a favourite of her mother's. Robyn had enthusiastically agreed.

She should have known better.

"Oh." Dad had met her eyes for a fleeting moment before looking down. "She had to go."

"Go?"

"Yes."

"Why?"

"On business. For a week. She caught the early plane. Taxi came at five this morning."

"And she didn't even bother–"

"The phone call came late last night. You were asleep. She said to say she's sorry, but that business–"

"Comes first. How silly of me to get my hopes up, to believe that for once she'd think her daughter was more important than her bloody business."

Tears had welled up in her eyes as she abruptly stood up.

"And you, as usual, did nothing to stop her."

"Robyn, that's not entirely–"

"You can eat it yourself!" she'd shouted angrily, thrusting her chair back and reaching for her school bag.

"Eat what?"

"Your golden-brown toast."

"Robyn, I'm sorry, but–"

His voice had been cut off as Robyn slammed the front door behind her.

Now she regretted shouting at Dad, but he'd been the only person available to direct her hurt and anger at.

Robyn sighed. She'd been let down by her mother, shouted at her father, crossed swords with the principal and been given detention. Could the day get any worse?

Chapter 4

The sound of footsteps made her turn round. Coming towards her was the tall athletic figure of William Saunders, carrying a gym bag with a pair of running shoes tied to the handle. William was captain of the athletics team, and they had got to know each other through their leadership positions in school sport.

"Hi, Robyn." William smiled as he stopped alongside her. "All by yourself?"

"What does it look like?" she snapped.

"Oh, sorry."

She immediately regretted her tone. Over the last few weeks she'd become increasingly attracted to William, always finding him friendly and easy to talk to.

"It's OK. It's my fault. I didn't mean to be rude."

"Bad day?"

"Yeah, you could say that. Had a run in with Smelly this morning. He's given me detention."

"Really? Bad luck."

She was mildly surprised when he sat down next to her and asked sympathetically, "What did you do?"

"Nothing. Yeah, I know everybody says that, but all I did was answer him back and didn't address him as 'sir'."

He smiled. "All you did was answer him back, eh, Robyn Howard?"

Robyn grinned back, feeling her angry mood disappearing in the warmth of his smile.

"I just wish he ..."

"What?"

"I wish he wasn't so negative. Every time he speaks to me, or anyone else for that matter, he's always complaining, always looking for ways to punish any student who disagrees with him."

"He's not that bad, Robyn. At times I've had to discuss the athletics programme with him and I've always found him to be OK."

"Huh, that's because you're a male."

"Oh, you've noticed," replied William with a smile.

"It's all very well for you, but he's never said *anything* positive to me, even though I'm a sports captain too. There's obviously only one reason for that."

"OK." He paused and smiled again, then picked up one of the leaves that lay scattered under the tree and began pulling it to pieces. "I didn't stop to talk to you about Smelly. I wanted to ask you something."

"What?"

"The school ball. It's coming up next month."

"Oh," replied Robyn, somewhat taken aback.

"I was wondering … that is, I was hoping … that you'd come with me as my date."

"To the school ball?"

"Yes. Has anyone else asked you yet?"

He reached out and took her hand. She was surprised at his touch, but made no attempt to withdraw it.

"No. Nobody has."

"Well then, will you let me take you?"

"Look," he said, when she didn't immediately reply. "I'm sorry for arguing with you about the principal. Your point of view has some merit, and–"

"Some merit?" responded Robyn angrily, pulling her hand away. "One minute you're asking me to the ball and the next you're patronising me. Obviously as a girl I don't have a brain."

"Robyn, that's just not fair." His eyes had lost their tenderness and now flashed with anger. "I asked you to the ball because I like you, and I thought–"

"You thought what?" It was more a challenge than a question.

"I thought I'd like to get to know you better."

Robyn tossed her head back. "Well now you have, and–"

"Yes, now I have." He locked eyes with her for a long moment before abruptly standing up. "And I'm not so sure I like what I hear or see."

William spun round, and without a backwards glance strode off towards the sports ground.

Robyn watched his receding figure until he turned a corner and disappeared from sight. Her mind was in turmoil. Her mother's let down, the confrontation and detention, and now she'd started a stupid argument with a boy she'd found interesting and attractive. She'd been surprised and pleased when he'd invited her to the ball, but her bad mood had got the better of her and now he'd gone. Tears of anger and disappointment filled her eyes.

She looked at her watch. She was due in detention in five minutes.

Could this day get any worse?

She sighed heavily, slowly rose to her feet and began to walk towards the main school building.

Chapter 5

Robyn paused outside the detention room. "Bloody detention," she muttered as she opened the door.

"What was that, Robyn?"

To her surprise she saw Miss Robinson sitting at the teacher's table.

"Oh, you're here, Miss Robinson."

"Yes. Looks like we both drew a short straw."

Robyn frowned. She knew the students hated detention, but had always assumed the teachers enjoyed supervising those being punished for bad behaviour.

"Well, you'd better find a seat and get on with your assignment."

Robyn looked around. The other students were watching her curiously – a senior girl, and a sports captain at that, was a rarity in the detention room.

Avoiding their gaze Robyn took a seat at the front of the room, unzipped her computer case and placed her laptop on the desk. As the screen lit up she opened a new document, typed *Famous Men in History*, and began to write.

Written English came easily to her, and she'd already decided to rely on her general knowledge, as History had always been a favourite subject. She'd work her way through the ages, and when she reached five hundred words she'd write a conclusion.

She'd begin with Julius Caesar. His conquest of Britain in 55 BC would use up plenty of words. What a pointless exercise!

Her loud sigh was involuntary.

"Something wrong, Robyn?"

Miss Robinson was not wearing her usual pleasant expression. She obviously felt it necessary to adopt a different persona when being detention supervisor.

"No."

"What's your assignment?"

"An essay."

Miss Robinson raised an eyebrow.

"I have to write about—"

A sudden burst of wind swept through the classroom window, scattering the papers on Miss Robinson's desk.

"Good grief! Where did that come from?" she exclaimed as she jumped up and slammed the window shut.

A rumble of thunder echoed in the distance as the sky darkened.

"Odd." Frowning, she switched on the classroom lights and turned back to Robyn.

"Now, what's your assignment?"

"I have to write an essay on the lives of three famous men in history."

"And you, of course, would rather be writing about …"

"Famous women in history. I've often dreamed of being a female leader, living a life of adventure and power."

"Well, dreaming is one thing. However, I'm not sure if–"

She was interrupted by a cacophonous clap of thunder that resounded through the room, causing all the girls to duck down. Slowly and cautiously, as the sound receded, the girls began to sit upright.

"It's all right, girls. Thunder can't hurt you. It just sounds scary."

Miss Robinson was obviously making an effort to look relaxed and confident.

A sudden eerie howl of wind made everyone flinch. It was instantly followed by sheets of driving rain and tattoos of hail beating on the classroom windows.

"What's happening, Miss Robinson?"

"Are we going to be OK?"

"It's only rain and hail, girls. There's no–"

A brilliant flash of lightning was immediately followed by a second ear-splitting detonation of thunder. The classroom was momentarily illuminated by an unearthly glow before the lights went out and they were plunged into total darkness.

Chapter 6

As the sky cleared and the rumbles of thunder died away, Robyn realised she was sitting on the ground with her back against a rough surface. She reached down and touched damp grass. Scrambling to her feet, she looked around.

The rough surface was the bark of a tall oak tree, its roots mingling with the leaf-covered grass. It had obviously been raining, and the oak had provided her with shelter.

She looked right and left, but all she could see was thick forest with a small path running near to where she stood. Controlling a growing sense of alarm, she held her breath and listened for any sounds that might provide a clue as to her new surroundings. But all she heard was birdsong, and the rustling of leaves in a gentle breeze.

Instinctively she wrapped her arms around the front of her body. Unfamiliar textures made her look down, and she saw that she was dressed in a dark green tunic, leggings and knee-high boots. Around her shoulders was a hooded cloak of rich brown. Her bewilderment increased as she again looked about her, seeing nothing familiar. In a conscious effort to calm herself she began to breathe slowly and deeply, noting that in spite of the startling change in her environment, she wasn't afraid.

A bird swooped past, calling loudly. She took a startled step backwards and felt something heavy on her left thigh. Looking down again, she saw that a large belt around her waist held a scabbard, from which protruded a handle. Taking hold of it, she drew out a short sword with a blade that glinted in the late afternoon sun.

Startled, she almost dropped the weapon, but then her grip instinctively tightened. She moved her hand from right to left, feeling the sword's weight, and then swung a few experimental strokes. It seemed surprisingly familiar, and she found herself lunging forward on the balls of her feet, rapidly slicing twigs and small branches off the oak tree. Stepping back to admire her handiwork, she became aware that her sense of bewilderment was easing a little. Looking up at the twisted gnarled branches of the tall oak, she decided to take the initiative.

She thrust her sword into its scabbard, reached for a sturdy lower branch and hoisted herself up, climbing until she was high above the ground. Relaxing in the crook of two branches she gazed out at the view. The forest seemed to stretch for miles, uninterrupted by any sign of human habitation. Turning her gaze westwards she saw the faint outline of tower-like structures silhouetted against the setting sun. Her eyes narrowed as she tried to make out more detail, but her concentration was interrupted by a series of distant shouts.

"Robyn!"

"Where are you, Robyn?"

"Robyn!"

She looked down. Four young women were approaching through the trees. They were about Robyn's age, and like her were dressed in tunics and leggings.

She watched as they came closer. The concern on their faces told her they were searching for all the right reasons. Her curiosity overcame any lingering doubts, and she rapidly descended the oak.

As the four girls reached the base of the tree, she dropped to the ground.

"There you are, Robyn," said the tallest girl. "We thought you might have got lost in the storm."

Robyn stared at the girl, surprised that she'd been addressed by name.

"Robyn?" repeated the girl. "Is something amiss?"

"Was it the storm?" asked a fair-haired girl.

"No," responded Robyn uncertainly. "I took shelter under the oak. Terrible storm though, wasn't it?" She looked at each of them, noting they were watching her with puzzled expressions.

"Never heard thunder so loud," continued the fair-haired speaker. "And the lightning! It lit up the whole forest."

"Indeed, Ellen," said a slightly built girl whose round dark eyes contrasted with her delicate facial features. "Then it stopped as suddenly as it started. Methinks dark deeds are afoot."

"Don't be a dolt, Willow. It was just a storm," replied Ellen.

"Aye, but we were still worried about you, Robyn," said Willow. "The storm was unusually strong. It's a sign from the heavens. Change is a-coming."

"Change? For the good?" Robyn asked. She was beginning to feel less disorientated by her surroundings and more in need of information.

There was silence in the group as Willow pondered the question. "We can't be sure exactly what, yet, but the storm was a clear sign that something momentous is imminent."

"So it hasn't already occurred?" asked Robyn.

"Why do you ask that, Robyn?" said Willow. "Do you know of any recent occurrence?"

"Willow often has foreknowledge of strange occurrences," said Ellen. "Do you think she may be wrong this time, Robyn?"

Robyn paused, realising the question was an important one. By their manner, she could tell the group saw her as a leader.

"No, Ellen," she responded slowly. "Willow may well be right. Let us hope that what she speaks of has a positive outcome."

She smiled at the group, who were all nodding silently in agreement.

Willow spoke again. "Whatever the signs are, we should be heading back to the camp, Robyn. The sun will be setting soon and dark Sherwood is not a safe place to be."

"Can't be too careful," said Ellen. "The blood-price on your head is not a joke."

"The blood-price?" responded Robyn unthinkingly. The identification of the forest as "Sherwood" had startled her.

"But you already know that, Robyn," replied Ellen, looking puzzled.

The tallest of the girls spoke up. "There's a blood-price on the head of *all* outlaws, and yours, of course, is the highest, Robyn. It's up to us to keep you safe."

"True, Little Joan," replied Ellen. "And as Robyn has often reminded us, we must all look after each other."

"Speaking of which, I'm hungry." The fourth girl was a young woman, with short dark hair. "We haven't eaten since breakfast, and–"

"Verily, Freya, it would do you no harm to go without food for a few more hours," said Joan.

"You had better take these, Robyn," said Willow, interrupting the amused murmur of agreement. She handed Robyn a bow and a quiver of arrows. "You left them behind."

Robyn carefully took the quiver. Noting how the others wore theirs, she quickly put it over her left shoulder then reached for the bow. She held it at right angles and tugged at the threaded hemp bowstring.

She smiled as she felt the strength of the sturdy yew branch from which the bow had been shaped. The touch was familiar and the potential power of the weapon was reassuring. Pointing it skyward, she pulled back the bowstring and released it, smiling as she imagined an arrow winging its way towards the darkening sky.

She turned to face curious stares. "Just practising," she said briskly.

"Time to start moving?" asked Joan.

"Of course, Joan. You lead the way."

Joan hesitated for a moment, but at a nod from Robyn she set off down the path. Realizing the others had expected her to lead, Robyn moved quickly alongside Joan, and the rest of the group immediately fell in behind.

As they walked, Robyn thought through what she'd learned in the past half hour. She was in Sherwood Forest with a group of young women who were classified as outlaws – outside the law. They seemed lively and confident, knew her by name and regarded her as their leader. Their clothes were similar, although she noted that her own hood was of a richer colour than theirs.

Sherwood Forest, outlaws, bows and arrows and a leader who wore a distinctive hood. Was she Robyn Hood, an outlaw leader of a band of women? Her heartbeat quickened with excitement as the idea developed. In spite of the price on her head, if this was some sort of new reality, she was starting to feel comfortable with it.

Chapter 7

There was a spontaneous and enthusiastic shout of welcome as they entered the clearing. The group of about forty young women gathered round the campfire came forward with cries of delight. Others emerged from huts around the perimeter and quickly joined them.

"Robyn! You survived the storm!"

"Thought you might have got waylaid or captured!"

"Welcome! Thrice welcome!"

The words were accompanied by warm hugs as Robyn and her companions gathered round the blazing fire. Next to it, slowly turning on a spit, was the roasting carcass of a deer.

"As you can see, we waited for you."

"Though hunger was gnawing at our bones."

The speakers were two bright-eyed twins.

Robyn gestured at the roasting deer. "Your work?"

"Yes, my arrow." One twin grinned at her sister. "Rosanne did assist me a little."

"Not entirely accurate, Robyn. It was I whom Eleanor assisted."

"It would seem, Rosanne and Eleanor, that your hunting skills are matched by your cooking ability."

"And methinks the venison is ready to serve," responded Eleanor with a smile.

"So, fellow outlaws," called Rosanne, "come, help yourselves."

Forming themselves into orderly lines, the outlaws moved forward, carving slices of deer meat with their daggers, adding wild mushrooms from large wooden platters.

Eleanor had moved quickly to bring Robyn a wooden plate with generous slices of venison garnished with large mushrooms.

"Wine, Robyn?"

"Wine?"

"Yes," responded an outlaw whose ginger hair glowed in the reflection of the fire "An hour after you left, our scouts reported a small entourage on the forest road led by a stout churchman. We relieved them of several bags of coins and a cask of wine."

"The churchman tried to tell Colleen that the money was alms for the poor," chimed in a pretty fair-haired outlaw.

"I pointed out that he'd already forcibly taken substantial coinage from the poor in the villages," continued Colleen. "Fay then informed him that we would be returning it to the rightful owners."

"My words did not seem to impress him," said Fay, a slightly built young woman with long dark curls.

"Where was he heading?" asked Robyn.

"To Nottingham. After we'd relieved him of his coins

and wine he cursed us roundly, shouting that the Sheriff of Nottingham would be informed of our crimes."

"The Sheriff of Nottingham," mused Robyn. "Not a popular man in these parts?"

"Surely you jest, Robyn. The man's a tyrant," said Fay.

Robyn smiled and hastily nodded. "Of course. I'd love to see his face when he hears the news."

Wooden goblets were passed round.

"A toast!" called Joan. "To the Sheriff of Nottingham."

"The Sheriff of Nottingham?" came the puzzled response from the outlaws.

"Yes," said Joan, grinning. "His generous gift will assuredly quench our thirst!"

The outlaws raised their goblets.

"To the Sheriff of Nottingham!" they chorused amid laughter.

The summer evening was warm, and after their meal the outlaws sprawled around the campfire discussing the day's events. Robyn joined in the chatter, but after a while, still coming to terms with her new situation, felt the need to be alone. She moved to the back of the group and quietly slipped away into the woods surrounding the camp.

For several minutes she walked along a narrow path that wound its way between the towering forest oaks. At the edge of a small clearing she stopped, and after a quick look round sat down at the foot of an oak tree, leaning back against its sturdy trunk.

After her initial confusion, Robyn was finding her new role as leader of an outlaw band increasingly interesting. She was looking forward to the freedom it would give her, and to the challenges that would come with the responsibilities of leadership. Yet … unsettling recollections of her previous life still crept into her mind; memories that were becoming increasingly blurred. Somehow she had become a different person but was also the same person. Her body was the same, as was her name. What did it all mean?

The snap of a twig made her whirl round, jump to her feet and draw the short sword that hung at her side. A figure moved on the edge of the track and Robyn, now fully alert, stood close to the oak with her sword at the ready.

As she watched, the figure stopped moving and called out.

"'Tis I, Robyn!"

Willow stepped out onto the path.

"Willow," said Robyn, lowering her weapon. "Did you follow me?"

"I did. I saw you slip away from the camp, and knowing that you were troubled I followed."

"How did you–?"

Willow held up her hand.

"Of course you're troubled. You have come from another place and another time, and that confuses you."

Startled by Willow's revelation, Robyn stared at her for a long moment before replying.

"Who else has knowledge of this?"

"No one. Only me, and that's where the knowledge shall stay." She smiled gently. "Aspects of your new situation concern you, do they not?"

Robyn paused. "Yes," she replied slowly. "I know that I am

in a different place and time, but I also know that I'm still me
– if that makes sense."

"It does," replied Willow, seating herself at the base of
the oak tree and indicating for Robyn to join her. "You've
accepted that you've come from another dimension in time,
yet you know little about the new person you've become, or
…"

"Or my background, my childhood, my family, how I
came to be–"

Again Willow held up her hand. Then she smiled, and
reaching forward, took Robyn's hands in hers.

"All of this will slowly be revealed to you during your
coming nights of sleep, and through incidents that will soon
befall you. Each morning you will wake with an increased
recollection of your years in Nottingham, of your family and
friends and your connection with Sherwood Forest. By the
end of each day your knowledge and understanding will be
considerably increased."

"You're sure?"

"I am. You have my word."

"How do you know?"

"If I knew the answer to that I'd be able to tell you," she
replied. "Where this knowledge comes from I know not. But
I can assure you that what I have said will come to pass."

Robyn squeezed her companion's hands.

"I'll accept that. It could be fun," she said with a grin

"It certainly could," said Willow. "Your very own bedtime
story."

Robyn nodded and then frowned. "I still have one question."

"Which is?"

"Why am I here? I'm beginning to accept that I've been transported to this time and this place. But the question is, why?"

Willow paused before replying.

"What I *can* tell you is that you have taken the role of a person who is linked to you through your bloodlines. As to why, all I know is that there is a definite purpose in all of this."

Her large dark eyes looked deeply into Robyn's. "You are aware of the injustices and the inequalities in our town and our nation?"

Robyn nodded.

"In your role as leader you may not be able to make changes overnight, but whatever happens you will make your mark and leave an example for others to follow."

Robyn opened her mouth to reply, but Willow raised her hand. Her words were soft but crystal clear.

"Robyn, I do know that all will be well with you."

"All will be well with me," whispered Robyn.

"Yes, Robyn. That I promise."

"Thank you, Willow."

She stood, and reaching down, pulled Willow to her feet and they embraced.

"Come," murmured Robyn. "The others will be wondering where we are."

The two outlaws walked together down the winding path, entered the clearing and sat down near the fire.

Colleen joined them.

"Robyn, there is another piece of news that we gleaned from the churchman's group."

"What news, Colleen?"

"There were only two soldiers in the party. They quickly surrendered their weapons when we surrounded them. After we'd relieved them of their money and wine, one of them muttered, 'Don't try this tomorrow, you witches, or you'll be sorry.' The other soldier quickly ordered him to be silent, but our curiosity had been aroused. We seized the talkative one and–"

"Pricked his throat with my dagger," continued Fay. "He babbled that some high-ranking personages would be travelling through this part of Sherwood tomorrow at about noon, on their way to Nottingham Castle."

"High-ranking personages," said Robyn thoughtfully. "Did he have any more information?"

"No," said Colleen. "He assured us he knew nothing more. We believed him and let him go with the rest."

"We should intercept them, Robyn."

The outlaw leader turned to see Willow at her side.

"We should, Willow?"

"Yes. The storm was a portent. We should act."

"But it could be an ill omen?"

"I think not, Robyn. We would be foolish to ignore it. If the soldier spoke the truth and high-ranking personages are coming, their train will be large and well guarded. If we decide to intercept them we will need to be well prepared."

The flickering flames from the fire were reflected in

Willow's eyes, giving them an uncanny appearance. Robyn stared into them, aware of the expectant silence as the others awaited her response. A smile flittered across Willow's face and she gave Robyn an almost imperceptible nod.

Feeling a sudden surge of confidence, Robyn leapt to her feet.

"Outlaws, I believe the opportunity for much booty will present itself on the morrow! Guards, to your usual places! The rest of you to your beds. I want everyone up early tomorrow morning – well fed, weapons in top condition, and ready for a day of rich pickings."

Chapter 8

"Robyn! The signal!"

Willow's touch on her arm prompted her to look up into the top branches of the tall oak tree. There she saw an outlaw waving her arm in acknowledgement of a signal from a more distant oak.

"Positions, everyone!"

The outlaws, each armed with bows, arrows and swords, quickly moved into their pre-arranged positions. It was an ideal spot – a clearing surrounded by trees at the end of a long section of road. At the entrance the road turned sharply, which invariably caused travellers to slow down.

Robyn, crouching behind a small grove near the edge of the road, heard distant sounds funnelled through the tree-lined corridor. She listened intently as the clatter of hooves, the clank of weapons and the sound of creaking told of a large group moving at a steady pace.

"Mounted soldiers and some form of wagon in the centre," whispered Robyn.

Willow, crouched by her side, nodded in agreement.

First to appear were two mounted horsemen. Fluttering from the tips of their lances were red-and-blue swallowtail flags emblazoned with golden lions and fleur-de-lys.

"The royal banner – the new king's coat of arms," murmured Willow in surprise.

Two horsemen led a cavalcade into the clearing. Behind the leaders were three more mounted pairs, which in turn were followed by four sturdy oxen pulling a strange wagon, a mounted soldier on either side. Bringing up the rear were three more pairs of soldiers.

Inside the wagon, which consisted of a cage on wheels, a pretty young woman wearing flowing garments was sitting on large cushions. Even from a distance it was clear from the woman's hunched shoulders and bowed head that she was taking no interest in her surroundings.

The slow plodding gait of the oxen determined the pace of the entire group. As they entered the clearing, the soldiers looked around then shifted uncomfortably in their saddles in the noonday heat.

Robyn watched closely as the last of the group cleared the trees. Willow squeezed her arm.

"Ready, Robyn?" she whispered.

Robyn smiled, feeling an inner strength from her companion's touch.

"It's time."

Robyn reached for the hunting horn that hung at her side. Putting it to her lips, she blew a sustained blast. As the sound died away it was replaced by a menacing hum as a volley of arrows showered down on the soldiers. Eight of them toppled from their horses and hit the ground with a series of heavy thuds. They lay still. Another, an arrow in his arm, fell backwards to the ground with his left foot still caught in its stirrup. His frightened horse bolted, dragging the cursing man with it.

One of the leading banner-carriers spurred his horse into a gallop, but a second wave of arrows cut him down. His lifeless body lay sprawled across the royal banner that had fallen on the dusty forest road.

His companion was luckier. Several arrows had lodged in his shield and he had managed to spur his horse ahead of the second volley. A small dust cloud followed the sound of hoof beats as he disappeared into the forest at the clearing's edge.

At Robyn's second blast the outlaws, swords drawn, swarmed down the hillside. Four soldiers of the rear guard tried to turn their horses to face their foe, but were quickly surrounded and dragged from their saddles.

The wagon lurched to a halt and the wagon driver, a wizened ill-dressed man, sat cowering in his seat, his whip lying on the road below him.

One of the two soldiers escorting the wagon threw down his weapon and raised his hands in surrender. But his companion spun his charger round and, lashing out with his sword, spurred his horse straight at the nearest group of approaching outlaws. Before the beast could reach full speed, Joan sprang forward, seized the bridle and dragged its head around. The horse's momentum, combined with Joan's weight, caused it to fall sideways, throwing its rider clear. Cursing but unhurt he scrambled to his feet, still clutching his sword. Breathing heavily he glared at the outlaws who encircled him.

"Look to the young woman in the wagon and take the remaining soldiers prisoner! Leave this one to me!" commanded Robyn.

She pushed her way through the circle and, sword in hand, stood facing the soldier. Unlike his fellows, he wore a tunic bearing a symbol of a white stallion.

Willow, moving quickly to Robyn's side, murmured, "Take care, Robyn. He's Sir Guy of Gisbourne, the Sheriff's right-hand man."

Nodding her thanks, Robyn took another step forward.

"Sir Guy of Gisbourne, I believe." She gave a mocking bow. "Welcome to the greenwood."

"Presumably you'll be that foul wench Robyn of the Hood." In spite of his predicament his voice was self-assured and arrogant. Scornfully he surveyed the circle of outlaws. "A witches' coven, no less. Burning at the stake would be too good for you she-devils."

"Raise your sword, Guy of Gisbourne. We shall see if the quality of your mettle matches the foulness of your mouth."

The flat of Robyn's sword smacked sharply into his upper left arm, causing him to curse and recoil.

"See, Sir Guy. Wenches can sting!"

With a snarl the knight sprang forward, aiming a slicing stroke at Robyn's neck. Bouncing lightly on the balls of her feet she sideslipped the sword and dealt his upper arm a second stinging blow.

His temper snapped and with a howl of rage he charged at

her, slicing the air with swift strokes. Stepping aside, Robyn thrust out her left leg, sending him sprawling face down, his sword spinning from his grasp. Gasping for breath he twisted his body round and tried to scramble upright, but was thrust backwards by Robyn's foot on his chest and her sword at his throat.

"Yield, you arrogant cur."

Sir Guy's dark eyes stared at her with undiluted hatred.

Her sword tip moved forward a fraction, pricking the skin at his throat.

"Yield now, or my face will be the last memory that will accompany you to hell."

"I yield." His voice was barely audible.

Robyn's blade advanced a fraction, drawing droplets of blood.

"Louder," she hissed.

Making a supreme effort, the knight shouted hoarsely, "I yield!"

"Get him on his feet and secure him firmly," Robyn commanded. "He's a rare prize."

She turned away and strode towards the wagon, where a group of outlaws was gathered round the beautifully dressed young woman. She regarded Robyn with a mixture of curiosity and fear.

"Th-thank you for, er, rescuing me," she murmured hesitantly.

Robyn nodded an acknowledgement.

The young woman looked at the scene around her. The soldiers, guarded by the outlaws, were regarding their captors with a mixture of loathing and fear. Some of the horses had galloped away, but the rest remained contentedly cropping grass. Several outlaws were engaged in the less-than-pleasant task of tugging arrows out of the lifeless soldiers.

"Who are you? Who are all these women? Where do you come from?"

Ignoring her, Robyn turned and called out, "Gather up anything of value, including the horses. Tie the soldiers' hands, rope them together and then blindfold them." She looked back at the wagon. The driver was still hunched in trepidation.

"Wagoner!"

His head jerked up and he looked at the outlaw leader apprehensively.

"No need to tarry. Proceed on your way!"

With an agility that belied his age, the man scrambled from his seat, retrieved his whip and quickly flicked his oxen into action. Cart, beasts and man rumbled forwards.

Robyn nodded towards the young woman. "Bring her. Now, all of you, let us away!"

The outlaws, the young woman and their bound and blindfolded captives moved quickly into the anonymity of the dark forest, leaving the remnants of their attack strewn around the clearing.

Chapter 9

"You're obviously from a family of substance, so tell us how you happened to be in the carriage under royal protection."

Robyn was seated on a large oak stump that had been cleverly fashioned into a chair. The rescued girl stood in front of her, watched by outlaws who were sprawled on the ground. Others were on guard duty around the perimeter of the camp, or outside the hut where the prisoners were held.

"Before I tell you, can you answer me one question?" replied the young woman.

Robyn noted that her voice was that of an educated person. "Possibly."

"The others call you Robyn. Are you the outlaw they call Robyn o' the Hood, Robyn Hood?"

"I am."

"I've heard about you, a band of outlaw women who defy the authority of the Sheriff." She hesitated and looked directly at Robyn. "I'd love to join you."

There was a murmur of amusement from the watching outlaws.

"Join us?"

"Yes. You probably think I'm from a privileged background."

"And you're not?"

"Yes, but no." The young woman's eyes flashed. "I'm trapped and manipulated. I have no say in what I do. It's all decided for me."

"By whom?" murmured Robyn, already anticipating the answer.

"By men. Powerful men. I'm a plaything, a political pawn. I have no power and my opinions are regarded as worthless." Her eyes moved across the group. "You're all outlaws, but at least you have some say in who you are and in your future."

"So you think joining us would be the answer to all your problems?" asked Robyn.

"T'would be a good start," replied the young woman emphatically.

"If you want to join our band you must pass some tests." Robyn paused. "Physical tests," she said with emphasis.

The young woman smiled. "I propose a bargain. Let me undertake your tests. Then, whether I pass or fail, I will tell you about myself and my circumstances."

"Sounds fair, Robyn," said Joan. "But we need to at least know her name."

"Indeed. So, what are you called?"

"Most people call me Pip."

"Then Pip it shall be. So, Pip, are you ready for the tests?" She gave the young woman a searching look. "We don't take just anybody, you know."

With a swift movement Pip unwrapped her long dress to reveal a short leather skirt.

"I'm game, Robyn. I'm not just anybody, you know."

Some of the band murmured in surprise, but Robyn continued briskly. "We have four contests in which you'll be matched with our champion, Joan." She smiled. "Sometimes known as Little Joan."

The outlaws cheered as Joan, a head taller than the rest, stepped forward.

"The first contest – the longbow!" called Colleen.

Robyn signalled and Colleen handed Joan a bow and arrow. She indicated a tree.

"It's forty paces from here. See the white mark on it? That's the target."

To shouts of encouragement Joan stepped forward, fitting an arrow to the string. She raised her bow and the outlaws fell silent. She paused and then released the arrow. All eyes followed its flight and then applauded loudly as it struck the target –dead centre.

With a smile of sympathy and a gentle shake of the head, Colleen handed Pip a bow and arrow. In rapid succession she raised the bow and fired. There was silence followed by a collective gasp of incredulity. Pip's arrow had split Joan's arrow in half.

"Hmm," said Robyn. "Had some practice, have you?"

Pip merely smiled.

"Next contest," called Colleen. "Unarmed combat!"

The outlaws quickly formed a circle, and Joan signalled to Pip that she should join her in the centre. Clearly peeved at the result of the archery contest, Joan spat on her hands, rubbed them together and rushed at Pip, aiming a blow that her opponent only partially evaded, causing Pip to stagger back. As the outlaws cheered Joan lunged again, but this time Pip swiftly stepped aside and clipped her with a blow that sent her onto one knee. Furious, Joan jumped up and, charging at Pip, managed to seize the front of her tunic with both hands. Pip immediately slipped her hands inside Joan's arms, knocked them apart, thrust her right foot behind Joan's left leg, thumped her chest and sent her sprawling backwards.

Robyn looked down with a reproving frown.

"You lose again, Joan."

Joan quickly scrambled to her feet.

"Robyn, that was just a lucky break. This time–"

"No, Joan, this time is my time." She turned to Colleen. "Swords!"

Colleen brought two swords forward.

As the outlaws called encouragement, the two circled each other warily. Robyn suddenly lunged forward but Pip parried the thrust. Pip then attacked with a series of blows that Robyn blocked, responding with a series of her own, also blocked by her opponent. They stepped back to catch their breath and then simultaneously lunged forward. Their swords locked together and both strove to gain the upper hand.

Making a supreme effort, Robyn put all her bodyweight behind a forward thrust, but Pip held her ground. Robyn's face was inches from Pip's and she could hear her opponent's hoarse intakes of breath that matched her own. Their eyes locked and Pip blinked as a trickle of sweat reached her eyelids.

"Had enough?" Robyn muttered, still maintaining the pressure.

"Only if you have."

"On the count of three we'll both step back."

Pip nodded. At "three" they both stepped back and, breathing heavily, lowered their swords to applause from the watching women.

Robyn stared at Pip for a long moment.

"Congratulations, Pip. You're full of surprises."

"Thanks. I'm really looking forward to joining your band."

"Just a minute," responded Robyn. "We had a bargain. Sit down and we'll continue where we left off."

There was an air of expectation as the outlaws quickly gathered round. Pip's prowess had added a sharp edge to their curiosity.

"So," began Robyn, "why were you a prisoner under the banner of King John?"

"I was being taken to the Sheriff of Nottingham by Sir Guy of Gisbourne."

"Why?"

"King John had given me in marriage to the Sheriff."

The outlaws chorused their revulsion at the idea of marriage to their sworn enemy.

"But why?"

Pip paused and looked round the expectant faces. "Because I'm King Richard's niece."

Robyn instinctively stood.

"Pip." She paused. "Princess Phillipa. Are you Princess Phillipa?"

"I am. My grandfather was King Henry II."

"So your father is …"

"Geoffrey Howard. He was King Henry's son – illegitimate son, but granted royal privileges."

Robyn hesitated before putting the next question.

"Do you have any brothers or any sisters?"

"I have only one older sister. But I haven't seen her in years."

"Why is that?"

"It's not really that important, and I–"

"It *is* important!" The vehemence of Robyn's response startled the outlaws. Then, barely whispering, she asked, "What happened to her?"

"She, um, she–"

"Yes?"

"She was charged with murdering the captain of the Sheriff's guard. She was arrested and locked up pending execution. But she escaped and disappeared."

"You say your sister was charged with murder. Was she guilty?"

Pip sighed and shook her head. "I never believed it was murder."

"Why not?"

"I was very young at the time. But everything I've heard about my sister makes it very hard for me to believe she was a murderer." She shrugged uncertainly. "Maybe it was self-defence. Nobody knows."

"*I* know," Robyn said softly, after a moment.

Joan broke the stunned silence.

"You know, Robyn?"

"Your sister was out riding when she came across the captain of the guard and two soldiers. They were tormenting a blind beggar. She ordered them to stop, but they refused. She repeated the order, whereupon they drew their swords and attacked her. She fought back and killed the captain. Your mother had died the year before and your father was fighting in the Crusades with King Richard. Realizing there was no one powerful enough to protect her she tried to escape, but the Sheriff of Nottingham's men hunted her down and she was locked up on a murder charge. She would have been tortured and hanged, but with the help of a sympathetic soldier she managed to escape and disappeared into Sherwood Forest."

Pip stared at Robyn. "How do you know all this?"

"What was the name of your sister?" The question hung in the air as every outlaw leaned forward.

"Robyn. Princess Robyn."

Tears streamed down the face of the outlaw leader. "Yes. Me."

The sisters fell into each other's arms, kissing and hugging to loud applause. Finally they drew back, but their arms remained linked.

"So you didn't murder the captain."

"No. I hated leaving you, but I knew that if I didn't escape, a painful death would be my inevitable end."

"I'm sure you're right. King Richard had been killed and

Father was reported missing in battle and was presumed dead, so the newly crowned King John took me as his ward. It was he who granted the request from the Sheriff of Nottingham for my hand in marriage."

"You had no say in it, of course."

"No say at all. I'm a mere woman – a chattel."

"Did you try?"

"I pleaded with King John but he wouldn't listen. He ordered me to go ahead with what he described as 'an advantageous union'. The Sheriff has been a close crony of Prince John for years, and he knew that marriage to me would make him an even closer ally of the new king."

"You're now safe from his evil clutches," said Robyn. She turned towards the outlaws. "Before the day is over, we have one more important task to perform. Joan!"

"Yes, Robyn?"

"Bring forth the prisoners and their …" she smiled, "transport."

Joan grinned. "With pleasure, Robyn."

The band members formed a large circle as Sir Guy and the soldiers, still bound and blindfolded, were led into the centre. Although the soldiers were subdued, their leader had recovered some of his courage. Twisting his head from side to side he began cursing Robyn and the outlaws.

Tiptoeing quietly forward Robyn stood with her face close to his.

"Boo!" she shouted.

Involuntarily he jumped back, stumbled and fell heavily, to loud laughter.

"Get him on his feet!" Robyn commanded.

Two outlaws hoisted him upright and Robyn resumed her stance near his face.

"Listen carefully, Sir Guy."

"Vile strumpet. I'll—"

"You'll do nothing if you know what's good for you. Be silent and listen."

His heavy breathing betrayed his anger, but he remained silent.

Robyn stepped back and raised her voice.

"All of you prisoners will be shown mercy and returned to Nottingham. Unlike the Sheriff and his minions, we do not beat or flog prisoners. That does not mean that we are weak. It shows that we are merciful, it shows that we are able to demonstrate a humanity that Sir Guy and his ilk are sadly lacking."

The knight could no longer contain himself.

"It shows that you're cowards; weak, pathetic women who have been lucky enough to capture a few soldiers and me. But, Robyn Hood, mark my words. There will be a day of reckoning when you and the others in your foul witches' coven will hang or burn as you deserve!"

"Clearly a refined and gentle knight such as you deserves a fitting form of transport," responded Robyn sarcastically. She signalled, and a small donkey was brought into the centre of the circle.

"An ass, Sir Guy."

The donkey gave a snort, lifted its head and brayed. The

outlaws laughed and applauded as Robyn again stepped close to Sir Guy's blindfolded face.

"To teach you to mind your manners when addressing ladies, you will be placed on the ass, facing its arse." She turned to Joan. "Up he goes."

Two outlaws seized the fuming knight and swung him backwards, facing the donkey's rear. To further laughter and applause his legs were bound tightly underneath its belly. A longer rope was tied round his waist and then used to link each of the soldiers together in a file behind Sir Guy and his new steed.

"Lead them out of the woodland onto the Nottingham road. Then remove their blindfolds and send them on their way."

"Remove their blindfolds, Robyn?" questioned Colleen.

"Yes. I want them to witness their humiliation as they reach the outskirts of the town. It's market day so there'll be large crowds on the road. Sir Guy and his band will provide them with much amusement."

She gave the donkey a light whack on the rear and it started forward.

"God speed, Sir Guy. Give our most humble salutations to the Lord High Sheriff."

The knight's curses were drowned in a jeering chorus as the procession began to make its stumbling exit from the clearing.

As the outlaws' laughter died away, Robyn called, "Back to the clearing. Time for a little celebration!"

In the clearing the women gathered round their leader as she called, "Willow, your harp. 'Tis time for our song!"

Willow, harp in hand, seated herself next to Robyn and strummed a lively introduction, then nodded to her fellow outlaws. With considerable enthusiasm they joined her in a rousing song.

We're the band of Robyn Hood
We live in the forest glen.
We fight for truth and justice
Against the Sheriff's men.
A female band of outlaws
We fight against our foes
With sturdy shields and broadswords
With arrows and with bows.

Chapter 10

Sounds of laughter and jeering floated up to the dining room of Nottingham Castle, where its chief resident, the Sheriff of Nottingham, was commencing his lunch.

"What's that infernal noise?" he enquired of his chief steward.

"No idea, my Lord Sheriff," replied the man with exaggerated courtesy.

The Sheriff snapped his fingers and pointed to the goblet on the table in front of him. For the third time the chief steward filled it to the brim with red wine.

"Would you like me to inquire, sir?"

The Sheriff paused in the act of spearing himself a generous portion of meat.

"Do that. I'm not used to hearing laughter at this hour, or at any hour in fact. And find out if there's any news on Sir Guy's escort train. They're well overdue."

"Yes, my Lord Sheriff."

As the man exited, the Sheriff took a generous gulp from his goblet. The delay of the escort train was increasingly worrying. Currying favour with King John had included agreeing to his demands for substantial monetary gifts, but once the negotiations had been completed and the marriage agreement signed, the Sheriff had been delighted. His investment had been well worth the effort. He would now have a lovely young girl as his bride. He wiped his black-bearded mouth, relishing the prospect. Furthermore, his political future would be enhanced, as the marriage would ally him closer to England's new king. He gave a grunt of satisfaction – money and time well spent.

The increasing noise in the town square below broke into his thoughts. Irritated, he strode to the balcony and looked down. The sight that met his eyes was the stuff of nightmares. Surrounded by a laughing, jeering crowd of citizens, a dust-covered Sir Guy of Gisbourne was making his ponderous way into the town square, roped, bound and facing backwards on a donkey. Behind him stumbled the remnants of his men-at-arms. Of the young bride-to-be there was no sign.

The Sheriff's roar of fury instantly silenced the crowd. Shouting, "Call out the guard!" he disappeared from the balcony, and less than a minute later emerged into the square.

"Move these churls back!" he bellowed.

The soldiers of the castle guard came lumbering out of the guardhouse and, using their lances, forced the crowd of people away from Sir Guy and his luckless companions.

"Cut this fool down!"

Two soldiers hurried forward. Cutting the leg ropes with their short swords, they assisted the knight from the back of the donkey. He attempted to stand upright, but his trembling limbs caused him to stagger and fall to the ground in front of his furious master.

"On your feet, you miserable cur!" commanded the Sheriff, seizing him by the front of his soiled tunic and dragging him upright. The Sheriff was a head taller than the knight, who was forced to crane his head upwards to meet the Sheriff's furious gaze.

"Where is the *girl*?" Each word was clearly enunciated.

"W-we were attacked, my Lord Sheriff, by–"

"Many, many women." This came from one of the soldiers. Having been released from their bonds they had quickly gathered round Sir Guy, hoping to explain their situation.

A second soldier eagerly interrupted. "We put down many of them, but the women were too strong for us."

"The women were too strong for us," mimicked the Sheriff in a high-pitched voice. "Oh, you poor boys. And I'm sure you fought very bravely."

"Very bravely," chorused the soldiers eagerly.

"Excellent." His smile was malevolent. "Now let's test your bravery a little further. Under the lash." With snarl of rage he turned to the captain of the guard. "Take these cringing curs away and have them flogged!"

The men were seized by members of the guard and, still babbling excuses, were thrust towards the guardhouse at lance point.

The crowd watched expectantly as the Sheriff turned towards the sorry figure of Sir Guy of Gisbourne.

"The girl?" His voice was soft with menace.

"A prisoner, sir. A prisoner of Robyn Hood and her cursed outlaws."

"You let that bunch of renegade whores capture a princess of royal blood? Call yourself a soldier? Call yourself a knight? Huh! Sir Guy the ninny knight."

The chuckles from the watching crowd caused Sir Guy to blush and twitch with shame and embarrassment.

"My Lord Sheriff, could we discuss this matter elsewhere? This is not appropriate—"

"Appropriate? Perhaps my deepest darkest dungeon would be more appropriate?" He thrust his face close to the sweating Sir Guy. "Well, sir knight?"

The knight dropped his voice to a harsh whisper. "Sir, it is not appropriate for us to talk like this within the hearing of the common people."

The Sheriff paused and nodded. To maintain his power he had to be seen to have the loyalty and support of men like Sir Guy who, in spite of today's fiasco, was a knight of substance and power.

He turned to his guard captain. "Disperse this rabble," he ordered.

As the soldiers moved quickly towards the crowd, the Sheriff turned to Sir Guy.

"And you," he hissed, "clean yourself up and report to my private quarters."

Chapter 11

It was a clean but subdued Sir Guy who entered the Sheriff's private quarters an hour later. Although the Sheriff outranked him, they had always worked closely together, consulting and agreeing on matters relating to taxes, law and order, and crime and punishment.

Sir Guy was well aware that the Sheriff of Nottingham was not merely some local official – he was the King's personal representative, responsible for the administration not only of Nottinghamshire, but a fair distance beyond. As Sir Guy yearned to expand his own private wealth and power, the Sheriff was a logical ally.

He alone knew the secret of the death of Eleanor, the Sheriff's first wife. Officially she had been a victim of the plague, but in truth had been secretly murdered by two soldiers, on the orders of her husband. Sir Guy himself had then killed the soldiers, thus ensuring that only two people knew the reality of her death. Although this knowledge gave him a certain power over the Sheriff, it also put him in a vulnerable position. As today's events had clearly shown, his privileged position was by no means secure.

"Sit down."

Eyeing the other man with care, Sir Guy seated himself. At a click of the Sheriff's fingers, the head steward appeared and poured two goblets of wine. The Sheriff passed one to Sir Guy, who visibly relaxed.

"My Lord Sheriff, I can explain–"

The Sheriff held up his hand. "What is important is the action we now take." He looked intently at Sir Guy. "We have two goals to accomplish."

"Two?"

"The rescue of my bride."

"And?"

"And the elimination of that band of outlaw women."

"I agree. How dare those–"

"We cannot allow this band to continue to survive," the Sheriff interrupted. "They are growing in number and disrupting the lawful passage of citizens through Sherwood Forest. If they are not exterminated immediately their rebellious behaviour could become widespread. These outlaw women are largely peasants. They cannot be permitted to start taking control from their rightful masters. Where will it end?"

"I've heard rumours that the band members are being taught to read."

"*Read?* They are illiterate peasants! How can they learn to read?"

"It's what people are saying."

"Then that's another reason for their destruction. If they learn to read for themselves they'll learn to think for themselves. The result would be unimaginable. We must act swiftly!"

He rose to his feet.

"Sir Guy, you are to travel to castles and manors throughout the shires and recruit troops to hunt down these outlaws. No knight or lord will want this outlaw plague developing in their midst. Once you explain the realities of the situation they will willingly contribute soldiers and weapons."

"With such a large force behind us, I'm certain we'll be able to seek out and destroy all of those vixen," replied Sir Guy eagerly.

The Sheriff's eyes narrowed. "With one exception," he said slowly.

"One exception?"

"Yes. Hunt all of them down, but bring me Robyn Hood alive."

"I understand completely, sir." He stood facing his master, his features filled with new confidence. "Leave it to me."

He bowed briefly and, eager to begin regaining his favoured position, quickly left the room.

Walking out to the balcony, the Sheriff looked down on the milling market day crowds. They were mostly common people dressed in greens and browns, talking and haggling over prices. Any one of them could be a supporter of the outlaws. Some could even be spies, checking on the movements of the castle garrison.

Although the Sheriff employed a number of informants, they had been unable to obtain any significant information as to the whereabouts of the outlaws' main encampment. The Sheriff suspected this was because the band had widespread support among the common people, but that his informants were too frightened to say so. Sherwood Forest covered a wide area, and although a large contingent of soldiers might eventually be able to track them down, it could take weeks. Stronger measures were needed.

Abruptly he turned from the scene below, re-entered his quarters and summoned his scrivener. The man quickly appeared with quill pen, inkbottle and parchment.

"You called, my Lord Sheriff?"

"I want the following proclamation issued throughout Nottingham and its environs."

"Certainly, sir." The scrivener dipped his pen in readiness.

The Sheriff began to dictate with slow deliberation. "Let it be known that any person, male or female, found giving any form of aid or comfort to the outlaw called Robyn Hood, or any member of her illegal band, shall be tortured and put to death …" He paused, then his voice rose. "By being burnt at the stake or hanged by the neck. No mercy will be shown."

He looked searchingly at the scrivener. "Do you think that's clear enough?"

"Absolutely, sir," replied the man quickly.

He finished writing, and with rapid movements began to collect up his pen, inkbottle and parchment.

"One more thing."

"My Lord Sheriff?"

"Let the words 'No mercy will be shown' appear in bolder lettering."

The scrivener nodded and repeated slowly, "No mercy will be shown."

Chapter 12

Pip's revelation of their sisterhood and the events that had occurred in their lives had triggered memories of Robyn's Nottingham childhood. Vivid dreams added to the pictures of her past.

It had been two years since their mother had died – a traumatic event for a fifteen-year-old. Due to her parents' royal status, Robyn had been made a ward of the Sheriff of Nottingham and given a small room in his castle. To her distress, her younger sister, Phillipa, had been sent to stay in one of King John's castles. Unable to understand at the time, she later realised that John, who hated his older brother Richard, was punishing the two girls for their father's close family connection with the late king.

Truth be told, Robyn hadn't had a close relationship with her mother, who'd been a lady of some importance in the town of Nottingham. The times they had spent together had been enjoyable but infrequent. In Robyn's early years she had become close to her father, and had therefore been greatly upset by the news of his death.

The Sheriff had shown no interest in her other than to assign her a tutor to assist with reading, writing and French. The tutor was elderly and had other duties, so her lessons had been irregular at best. Seeking relief from boredom, she had joined the older women when they met to weave their tapestries, but she'd found their conversations tedious.

There had been no one else of her age in the castle, and consequently she'd become increasingly restless. Although she was not permitted into the castle grounds without a chaperone, one spring morning on an impulse she'd descended a spiral staircase, opened a large wooden door and cautiously stepped outside. There had been no one about, so she'd headed in the direction of a large inner wall to see what lay beyond.

Sounds of clashing and shouting immediately attracted her attention. Cautiously she approached the edge of the wall and peered round.

In a grassed area, six young squires were practising in pairs with short heavy wooden swords and shields. A tall dark squire was shouting advice and encouragement as he moved among them.

"Vary the blows! Watch your opponent at all times! Footwork, Edmund! Are your feet made of stone?"

Fascinated, Robyn moved to the edge of the grass. She'd seen plenty of men-at-arms moving about the castle, but had never seen them learning their craft.

Abruptly the squire called, "Halt!" and they all stepped back, breathing heavily. Taken by surprise, Robyn quickly turned back towards the wall's edge, but her movement caught the eye of the squire.

"Hey! You!"

Robyn's first instinct was to flee, but she found herself turning slowly to face the young men.

"Yes?" she responded, managing to keep her voice steady.

The tall squire advanced towards her.

"What are you doing here, girl?"

"Watching you practise."

"Why?"

Although his manner was offensive, Robyn chose to remain calm. "I've never seen these skills practised before." She forced a smile. "You all fight very well."

"You are not permitted here!"

"Why not?"

"You're a woman."

Robyn smiled. "Your powers of observation do you credit, good sir."

The chuckle from his companions increased his belligerence.

"This is no place for a woman." His voice rose in anger. "The arts of war are solely for men."

"Who says so? The law? The Church?"

He looked nonplussed for a moment, and Robyn seized the opportunity.

"You are all highly skilled, but I'm sure I too could learn." She paused. "If you'll give me a chance."

"You?" he responded scornfully.

"Why not, William?" called a fair-haired squire. "Give her a chance."

The others joined in a chorus of agreement. Robyn strongly suspected they were hoping to make a fool of her, but she stood her ground.

Without taking her eyes off William, she bent down and reached between her legs for the back of her long dress, pulling it forward and tucking into her waistband.

"So, William," she said, pointing at his sword. "Be good enough to show me how to hold this weapon."

His dark eyes met hers for a moment, then he shrugged and smiled mirthlessly.

"Be it on your head, fair damsel." He held the sword's hilt towards her and she wrapped her right hand round it.

"No, not like that," he barked. Moving alongside her he covered her hand with his. At his touch Robyn caught her breath and instinctively turned her head to meet his eyes. He held her gaze briefly then looked away.

"Let it go!" he commanded roughly.

Robyn slackened her grip.

"Like this. The blade should be held in an upright position."

He adjusted the sword and then closed her hand around the hilt.

"There." His hand lingered round hers for a moment before he released his grip.

"Edmund! Your sword," he commanded.

One of the young men tossed his sword towards William

who deftly caught it in his right hand. He took up an attacking stance alongside Robyn.

"Follow my lead!" he commanded with a hint of a smirk.

Robyn moved her right foot and shoulder forward, imitating his stance.

"Forward!" he commanded, thrusting the blade of his sword straight from the shoulder.

Robyn responded.

"Harder and with more speed."

Concentrating hard, she thrust her right arm forward, throwing her weight onto her right leg.

"Now back!"

He stepped back and Robyn followed.

"Don't lower your sword. Keep it at the ready position."

Robyn obeyed.

"Now with me. Forward! Back! Forward! Back!"

Quickly falling into the rhythm of the drill, she began to concentrate all her effort into increasing the speed and power of her thrusts.

"Halt!"

She stepped back, breathing heavily but maintaining her sword in the ready position. A burst of applause from the squires lifted her spirits. She turned to William. "Thank you. You're a good teacher."

"You're better than I thought you'd be," he conceded. He looked round the group. "That completes the practice for today. Gather your weapons."

Robyn took a step forward, looked into his eyes and placed her hand on his arm.

"William. Could I come again?"

"But, you–"

"Forsooth, William, where's the harm?" said Edmund.

Robyn noted that William had made no attempt to withdraw his arm.

"Very well. But–"

"But?" she enquired.

"Tell no one of this. No one," he emphasised.

"Of course not."

He nodded. "Then return on the morrow, at this time."

She gave him her warmest smile before she turned and, aware that seven pairs of young male eyes were watching her, walked slowly away.

A succession of lessons followed, in which Robyn learned the art of swordplay and the use of the shield. The squires also took her to the archery butts where she quickly learned basic longbow skills. Her good humour and enthusiasm endeared her to the entire group, and they took turns at keeping watch and concealing her from the occasional passer-by.

William was her main instructor, and most of the time he maintained a puzzling aloofness. Yet occasionally he displayed a measure of genuine concern and affection for her.

One day, when they were practising in pairs with sword and shield, he selected her as his opponent. Once the swordplay commenced he inexplicably launched an attack on her with such speed and ferocity that she was immediately knocked to the ground. Instantly he became contrite. Kneeling down and reaching out his hand, he gently pulled her upright and wrapped her in his arms. Although upset and angry, she was stirred by the feel of his heartbeat and his long heavy breaths.

"Robyn," he stammered. "Robyn, I–"

"I'm unharmed, William."

He continued to hold her.

"I know you didn't mean it, William." She looked up at him, and their eyes locked together.

Abruptly he released her and stepped back.

"Pick up your sword. You're matched with Sigmund." He indicated the smallest of the squires. "He's more your type."

Avoiding her bemused stare he quickly moved away.

Several similar incidents, when he was friendly – even tender – before turning away with a curt comment, left Robyn puzzled and angry.

In spite of William's unpredictability, she found herself increasingly attracted by his tall stature and dark-eyed features, and on the rare occasions when he laughed spontaneously or spoke words of praise or tenderness, her heart would skip a beat. However, when he rebuked her she felt only anger at his unfairness.

Late one afternoon, with practice over for the day, the squires began gathering their weapons.

"We're leaving shortly, Robyn." Edmund's forced casualness was puzzling.

"That's obvious, Edmund. I'll see you all tomorrow."

"For the last time." The voice was William's.

She turned and stared at him. He met her gaze then lowered his eyes.

"We're all leaving." His voice was low. "There's a rebellion in the north. Our services are required."

"Rebellion? Fighting?" Robyn tried to keep the fear from her voice.

"Yes."

Some of the squires were smiling in anticipation of actual combat, but William was subdued. Abruptly he turned to the others. "Leave us!" he commanded.

Several hesitated, but their more perceptive companions pulled them away.

Robyn and William stood alone in the clearing.

"Robyn, I–"

"Why didn't you say? You must have known for days. Why?" Her lips quivered with anger and distress. "Damn you, William. All this time and you said nothing."

His strong arms suddenly enveloped and nearly smothered her. She trembled but made no effort to struggle free.

"Robyn, surely you know."

"Know what, William?" she replied softly.

"That I care for you deeply."

"And I you."

They stood wrapped together, in silence.

"William?"

"Yes?"

"If you care for me so deeply, why do you criticise me so often?"

"Robyn, you're a lovely young woman, yet you are mastering the arts of war. How can I ...?"

"How can you what? Love a young woman who shows these skills?"

She pulled back a little and lifted her head to meet his gaze.

He hesitated and then softly replied, "Your knowledge and skills are a challenge to my–"

With an effort she broke free.

"Is that it? You think I'm a challenge to you? You think that because I'm nearly as skilled as you, I'm unworthy of your love?"

"No, that's not it. It's just that I can't understand–"

"You don't *want* to understand!" Robyn was trembling with anger. "It's clear to me that although you may care for me, you see me as a threat to your manhood."

"A threat to my manhood?" he spat.

The fierceness of his response caused her to step back. He advanced towards her until his face was inches away.

"God's wounds, that's absurd," he said.

Their eyes locked and their faces moved closer. They were both trembling. Robyn could feel his breath as his dark eyes searched hers. His face moved fractionally closer and lingered for a tiny moment, before he abruptly pulled away.

"You, lady, are no threat to me."

He spun round and strode from the clearing.

As the tears welled in her eyes, Robyn sank to her knees.

Chapter 13

The wild flower settled gently on the surface of the flowing stream and was borne swiftly away.

"Off on a new adventure," said Robyn, watching the flower she'd dropped into the water disappear from sight. "To where, only God knows. Rather like us."

The following morning, the sisters, still with much to talk about, had left the camp, and after walking for an hour were resting by the side of the River Idle, which flowed through Sherwood Forest.

Pip smiled and briefly took her sister's hand.

"I have no idea what the future holds, but I do know that I'm happier now than I've ever been. I've found my long-lost sister and a new freedom in this beautiful forest."

"It gets cold in winter," said Robyn, smiling.

"A minor inconvenience."

"An all-woman band. It's an original idea," said Pip.

"It is. Female fighters for freedom."

"So how did it start? Where did you all come from?"

"We're a mixed group – commoners, merchant class and

even a few from the fringes of nobility. We've joined for various personal reasons, but we all have one immediate goal." Her eyes blazed briefly. "The overthrow of the Sheriff's tyranny and the establishment of a just society with equal rights for all – men and women."

"Sounds very noble, but ..." Pip hesitated.

"Impossible?"

"Well, not entirely, but it is a daunting task."

"Yes, but we can't just stand by and do nothing. When I lived in the castle, I became friendly with some of the young squires, who showed me basic skills with the bow and broadsword. Since that time, here in the greenwood I've had more opportunities to develop my skills and pass them on to others." Robyn paused and looked at her sister. "What about you? Your skills with the longbow and sword are exceptional."

"A similar story to yours. I had a tutor in the castle in which I was confined, but he was too fond of sampling the ale supplies so I used to leave him asleep and wander around the castle grounds. One morning I encountered a young squire called Edmund, who spoke kindly to me. His father was a knight in the King's retinue. I was only fifteen then, but advanced physically for my age, and I think he–"

"Found you pleasing?"

"I believe so." Pip smiled at the memory. "We started meeting secretly and, like you and William, he began to show me longbow and sword skills."

"And nobody tried to intervene?"

"No. Another squire did find out about us and went to my tutor, hoping to cause trouble."

"The cur."

"It was to no avail. I told my tutor that if he reported me, I would report his drunkenness. It worked. He kept his mouth shut and I kept improving my skills. I was happy, until King John arrived at the castle and summoned me into his presence." She shrugged. "You know the rest."

"Were you able to see Edmund before you left?"

"Yes. I sent word to him through a trusted servant and we met for the last time by the castle wall. He was devastated, and confessed he'd harboured thoughts of a future for us together."

"And you?"

"I'd long suspected he might ask for my hand. Now that he'd confirmed it, I too was terribly downcast. I started to cry and he took me in his arms and with infinite tenderness kissed me." She paused wistfully at the memory. "Robyn, it was the most beautiful thing that had ever happened to me. Then we heard the perimeter guard coming so we had to part." She gave a long sigh. "God, how I miss him!"

"The prospect of marrying an evil churl like the Sheriff must have been even harder, after that."

"It was. My guardian saw how downcast I was and ordered me to be kept under twenty-four-hour watch." She smiled. "God's truth, your rescue was like a miracle. I know I've lost Edmund, but I've found my sister." She squeezed Robyn's hand. "But you still haven't told me how your band was formed."

"When I started to become proficient with weapons, I began thinking about the role of women," said Robyn. "I'd proved to myself I could reach a man's level of skill in spite of being female. Yet, women are regarded as inferior to men in all areas. We have no rights, and once married we become the property – the chattels – of our husbands."

"Nothing new in that."

"But it can be changed. I started off by talking to some of the other young women in the castle and marketplace. Some just laughed and said nothing could be done, or that the place of women was ordained by God. But others agreed with me. Some were from wealthy homes; others had fairly miserable lives with constant toil and little time to themselves. All shared a common frustration – their lack of control over their own lives."

Pip smiled mirthlessly. "I can relate to that. So then what happened?"

"I was already forming the idea of a group or band who could somehow work together to bring about change, when …" she paused and her brow darkened, "there was an execution – a death by fire."

"A burning at the stake?"

"Yes. In our town there was an older woman called Mistress Fletcher. She was a healer; she used to mix potions from herbs that she would apply on wounds and boils, or prepare as medicinal drinks. One winter's night four wolves, probably starving, attacked and killed three children in front of her home on the edge of the town. At church the following Sunday the priest claimed that the wolves were the servants of Satan, and had committed the dreadful deed because there was sinfulness in the town."

"Entirely logical, of course," said Pip sarcastically.

"Unfortunately the people believed him, and with mounting hysteria started babbling about seeking out a scapegoat. A woman whose child had recently died, in spite of Mistress Fletcher's efforts, claimed the healer was a witch and had caused the child's death. The priest eagerly supported her accusation of witchcraft. He informed the Sheriff who sent his men at the head of a mob to drag Mistress Fletcher out of her house and throw her in the castle dungeon."

"Poor wretch."

"The next day the townspeople were informed that the unfortunate woman had confessed to the crime of witchcraft."

"Under torture, of course."

"Of course. Three days later we were all ordered into the town square to witness 'the burning of a witch'. The nobles and officials were seated on a viewing platform or on nearby balconies while the rest of us were packed into the town square. It was a cold bleak day and we were all dressed as warmly as possible. Not so Mistress Fletcher."

"How do you mean?"

"At midday a shout went up from the balconies, and through the crowd I saw the poor woman dressed only in a thin white shift. Shackled by the wrists and ankles, she was half-carried, half-dragged along by two soldiers, supervised by the captain of the guard. She was shaking violently from either cold or fear."

"Or both."

"There was a tall stake in the centre of the square surrounded by piles of wood. Mistress Fletcher was hauled forward and forced hard up against the stake and tied tightly to it with a chain. The soldiers then moved back as the executioner, his head and face covered by a black hood, stepped forward. When Mistress Fletcher caught sight of him, she started to call for mercy."

"But there was none to be had."

"None at all. Some of the men on the balconies started shouting to the executioner to hurry up and light the fire. Some in the crowd joined in their calls, but many, particularly the women, hid their faces. It was hideous, Pip! The executioner ignited the wood and the flames started to lick at the base, and as they slowly crawled up her body her head twisted and turned in agony. It took her a long time to die."

Robyn paused, deeply disturbed by the memory. "I can still hear her screams."

The two sat in silence for a long moment before Pip asked, "What happened as a result?"

"The burning of Mistress Fletcher was supposed to frighten the people into greater obedience to the Church and the authorities. Yet it also showed the women of the town that females had no rights and no access to justice, and that they could be horribly executed at the whim of a male priest or sheriff."

Robyn gazed into the eddying waters of the river.

"Occasionally I was allowed to go riding outside the castle

walls. It was two weeks after the burning when I came across the captain of the guard and his cronies tormenting the blind woman. Their cruelty and the memory of Mistress Fletcher's death drove me to a fury. An attack from a woman was the last thing the soldiers expected." She smiled grimly. "You know the rest."

"You said they hunted you down and locked you in Nottingham Castle."

"Yes, in a cold and filthy prison cell." She shuddered at the memory.

"But you escaped. How?"

"It was late at night. They'd beaten me and I was in pain. Trying to sleep on the cold cell floor was virtually impossible, but eventually I managed to doze off. Then I was woken by the sound of someone opening my cell. It was dark, and I assumed the soldier standing in the doorway had come to beat me … or something worse."

"You must have been terrified."

"He advanced towards me, and I was about to scream when–"

"When what?"

Robyn smiled. "The moonlight shining through the cell window fell on his face."

"You knew him?"

"It was William, the squire."

"But I thought–"

"So did I. But he quickly explained that he was home on leave. He'd heard how I'd been locked up and had come to help me escape."

"From Nottingham Castle?" exclaimed Pip.

"Yes. I couldn't believe it. He helped me to my feet, and although I was bruised, fortunately nothing was broken. He then covered me with a soldier's cloak that he'd brought, put a helmet on my head and handed me a spear."

"Surely he didn't expect you to fight your way out?"

Robyn smiled. "No. He anticipated that I'd have been beaten, so told me to support myself with the spear. I tried it out and managed to move slowly but reasonably convincingly. He whispered that we should quickly leave the cell and walk down the passageway towards a half-hidden entrance – probably one they used to bring in poor wretches who'd been secretly arrested."

"What about the guards?"

"William said he'd taken care of them. I didn't ask what he meant as I was too busy concentrating on walking down the passageway. When we reached the entrance he unlocked the door and slowly opened it. I was very nervous, and I remember that when the gate creaked loudly, I grabbed William's arm for support. He smiled down at me, put his arm across my shoulder, kissed my forehead and steered me through the entrance."

"A little romance to go with the tension," said Pip, smiling.

"True, although I was too sore and tense to take much notice. We made our way across the grass towards a small gateway the outer wall. He led me through, and I got a fright as I came out the other side."

"Why?"

"There was a horse tethered to the wall. I thought we'd

been discovered. I couldn't help a small scream, but William clamped his hand over my mouth and told me quietly that the horse was his. I felt pretty stupid, but–"

"Understandable under the circumstances."

"I suppose so. Anyway, he lifted me up behind the saddle, mounted the horse and we cantered away."

"Where did he take you?"

"To the edge of Sherwood. We stopped near a river where he helped me dismount. I was still sore – the horse ride didn't help. He gave me the bags that had been strapped to the saddle; they had clothes and food inside. And he gave me a sword, a bow, and a quiver full of arrows."

"What happened next? Did he just leave you to it?"

Robyn shrugged and smiled. "He told me I was under sentence of death and had to escape into the forest."

"He didn't offer to come with you?"

"No, although I could see it wasn't easy for him. He said he'd heard of other women who had fled the town because of the burning of Mistress Fletcher. They were rumoured to be hiding in Sherwood, and he said I should try to find them. Dawn was starting to break, and he was becoming increasingly nervous. He said if I needed help, he'd come back to this place in a week's time."

"Big of him," murmured Pip.

"Yes, but I've thought about it since, and I realise William risked his life to save me. If they'd caught him he'd have been put to death. He took an enormous risk."

"I suppose you're right. But why?"

"Why what?"

"Why did he do it? He wasn't your lover. You said the last time you'd seen him you'd quarrelled and he'd stalked off."

"Before he left this time, he took me in his arms. I looked into his face and felt tears in my eyes – tears for the pain, the uncertainty and the fact that he was going to leave."

"Which he did."

"Yes, but he kissed me passionately first."

For a while neither of them spoke.

Softly, Pip asked, "Did you ever go back to the place by the river?"

"No. I was sorely tempted, but it was too close to the edge of the forest and I knew they'd be looking for me."

"And I suppose by then you'd already found the other Nottingham women."

"Yes, quite quickly in fact. They had a camp nearby. We all agreed we should go deeper into Sherwood and establish a more permanent camp – one that we could guard." Robyn smiled. "You know the rest."

"And William?"

"Who knows? He's probably betrothed to the daughter of a lord and has forgotten his brief dalliance with an outlaw wench."

"I think not, Robyn."

"Well, nothing can be done under these circumstances. I've got other priorities. But ..." she paused.

"But?"

"I still think of him and wonder what would have happened if–"

"If?" echoed Pip.

Robyn shrugged and shook her head. "My other priorities include the responsibility for a leading growing band of outlaw women."

"And what do you hope to achieve?"

"Increased self-confidence in each woman – through activities such as our reading classes. We then intend to pressure the authorities from a position of strength to bring about changes that will give women the same rights as men."

"What do you mean by pressure"?

"Force of arms if necessary, or negotiation – probably the first, followed by the second. I'm sure it can be done. We just need time and dedication."

"And meanwhile?"

"Meanwhile," said Robyn, lying back on the grass, "we have this beautiful forest to provide us with rest and inspiration."

Shafts of sunlight filtering through the canopy of oak leaves made dappled patterns on the ground. Robyn was about to close her eyes when she heard a slight sound. She turned her head to her left, expecting to see a deer, but saw nothing. Frowning in puzzlement, she looked to her right. To her horror, four armed soldiers suddenly burst through the trees and came running towards them.

"Robyn!" screamed Pip.

A second group of four crashed into the clearing on her left.

"Back to back!" shouted Robyn, scrambling to her feet and drawing her short sword.

The two young women moved rapidly into position and faced the advancing soldiers, who slowed their approach.

"Well, look what we've got here," called the leading soldier. "Two lovely little birds and none of their mates within squawking distance."

He swung at Robyn, who blocked the blow and retaliated with a swift movement that opened a wound in the man's right arm.

"Outlaw bitch! You'll pay for that. Get them!"

The other seven advanced warily. One of them swung a blow at Pip who deflected it and thrust her sword into his left thigh. He staggered back, clutching his bleeding limb.

"Step back, men. The vixens fight well. Let's wait for the others."

"Others," muttered Robyn. She suddenly thrust her arm upwards, pointing her sword above the men's heads.

"Here they come!" she shouted.

Instinctively the soldiers whirled round. Robyn immediately lifted her hunting horn to her lips and blew two blasts.

With shouts of anger the soldiers turned back to the young women. Swords flashed and clashed as Robyn and Pip sought to contain the collective attack of the six men-at-arms.

As Pip ducked a sweeping blow aimed at her head, a sword thrust in her right arm caused her to drop her sword and stagger sideways. Immediately she was knocked to the ground. Two soldiers dragged her away while the others circled the outlaw leader.

"Remember our orders – take her alive," ordered one of the soldiers. "But let's have some fun first."

"One woman against four of the Sheriff's goons," muttered Robyn. "Pretty even odds."

She was in open space with nothing and no one to protect her back. Balancing on the balls of her feet, she twisted and turned with cat-like grace and speed.

"Come on you buffoons!" Her sword flashed and the men stepped back. "Four men against a mere woman. You're pathetic."

Angered, one of the soldiers shouted, "Altogether mates! All of us! Attack!"

The two soldiers guarding Pip swiftly joined their fellows in a concerted circular attack. Robyn's retaliation rate increased and her sword's lightning thrusts and parries seemed to come simultaneously from a dozen different positions. Yet the odds against her were too high. While engaging three of them, a fourth came from behind and dealt her a heavy blow to the head with the hilt of his sword. She collapsed to the ground as the men circled round her with triumphant shouts.

"Get her on her feet!"

Two soldiers roughly dragged her upright.

"Where's the other vixen?"

The men looked round. In the latter stages of the fight, Pip had managed to scramble unnoticed out of the clearing into the shelter of the forest.

"We need to find–"

"No we don't. This is the prize we came for. Her other wenches could be here at any moment. Come on!"

The soldiers needed no further urging. Assisting their wounded comrades they headed back into the forest, dragging with them the semi-conscious outlaw leader.

Chapter 14

It was the jolting that caused Robyn to stir. She tried to move her arms, but realized there were heavy shackles on her wrists. Looking down she saw that her ankles were similarly fastened.

She carefully raised her throbbing head and looked around. Her vision cleared enough for her to see that she was confined inside the same cage on the ox cart that had been Pip's prison transport. This time, however, the armed escort was much heavier. The cart was flanked by three ranks of foot soldiers and two further ranks of mounted soldiers. The constant rattle and clank of their weapons, combined with the clumping of the soldiers' boots and horses' hooves, made it impossible for Robyn to hear anything else. Through the press of men and horses she was able to catch brief glimpses of trees and the occasional dwellings. She assumed they were on the main road through Sherwood en route to Nottingham.

Not wishing to attract the soldiers' attention, Robyn slumped into a resting position and half-closed her eyes. Clearly her situation was desperate. The escort was numerous and heavily armed, and therefore her chances of being freed by an outlaw band attack were severely limited. Speculating on the reason for being captured alive, she quickly realized she would almost certainly be tortured and executed as an example to others. She shuddered, and tried to dismiss the horrific images that began to crowd her aching head. Eventually the combination of the rocking motion of the cart and her semi-dazed condition lulled her into an uneasy sleep.

"It's Robyn Hood!"

"Robyn Hood the outlaw! She's been captured!"

The shouts woke her, and peering between the soldiers and horses she saw people lining the roadside on what appeared to be the outskirts of the town. Some were running alongside her cart trying to catch a glimpse of her, but the mounted soldiers were forcing them away with blows and curses. Clearly they were under orders to ensure their prisoner arrived safely in Nottingham.

"Obviously I'm regarded as a personage of some importance," thought Robyn wryly.

Her head had almost cleared, but she remained in a slumped position, monitoring her progress through narrowed eyes. Occasionally a foot soldier would peer into her mobile prison cell and mutter, "The bitch is still asleep," or something equally flattering.

As they approached the centre of town the crowds became bigger and noisier. The pace began to slow, and Robyn felt the wagon negotiate several corners on the cobbled streets before coming to a halt. As the flanking horse soldiers wheeled away, Robyn could see they had reached Nottingham's town square.

Orders were shouted and her cage door was opened. Two soldiers reached in and roughly pulled her out. Eight others quickly encircled her.

Word of her capture had obviously spread rapidly, as the square was a seething mass of people. Looking up she saw that a large platform had been erected at one end of the square, on which a table and several chairs had been placed. On the right-hand side, silhouetted against the blue sky, was a gibbet, its noose hanging menacingly. Robyn shuddered.

But she had little time to contemplate the scene as a shout suddenly went up from the crowd. "The Sheriff!"

Advancing up the steps to the platform Robyn saw two familiar figures – the Sheriff of Nottingham, followed by Sir Guy of Gisbourne. Both men strode to the platform centre and stood glowering at the crowd. The Sheriff's expression was one of cruel satisfaction. Sir Guy, standing slightly behind him, was also smiling grimly.

"Bring the prisoner!" The Sheriff's voice rang out across the square, silencing the assembled citizens' excited babble.

Robyn was propelled forward by the phalanx of soldiers who roughly cleared a path through the crowd. The shackles on her feet made progress difficult, but she had already determined to hold her head high and put on a brave show.

When she reached the foot of the steps, it was clear that with shackled feet she'd be unable to climb. In response to an inquiring look from the escorting soldiers, the Sheriff gave a thin smile.

"Unshackle the prisoner!" He looked at the formations of soldiers ranged in front of the platform and surrounding the crowd. "Escape is impossible."

The shackles were removed and Robyn was ordered to climb the steps. She mounted each one with deliberate slowness. When she neared the top she paused, turned to look back at the crowd, clenched her right fist and thrust it high in the air.

There was an immediate outburst of cheering and a chant of, "Robyn! Robyn! Robyn Hood!"

"Silence!" bellowed the Sheriff, incensed at Robyn's boldness and the crowd's reaction.

The soldiers instantly lowered their lances, pointing them menacingly at the assembled people. The cheering was reduced to an excited buzz of anticipation.

"Step forward, outlaw!"

Robyn mounted the final step and walked boldly towards the Sheriff.

"That's far enough, wench," commanded Sir Guy, who had moved quickly across Robyn's path.

The outlaw leader paused and gave a slight bow.

"Sir Guy of Gisbourne," she said loudly. "The last time we met you were facing the arse end of an ass."

The wave of laughter caused the knight to take an involuntary step back, enabling Robyn to move closer to the Sheriff. She frowned. This was the first time she'd actually seen the man, yet the menacing hunch of his shoulders and the forward thrust of his head seemed strangely familiar.

Clearly trying to keep his temper, the Sheriff advanced to

confront her. Several soldiers quickly started forward, but the Sheriff waved them back. She moved towards him until they were eyeballing each other, so close she could see the hairs in his left nostril moving as he breathed heavily. His head moved back a fraction and he smirked.

"Well, if it isn't Robyn Hood, the fearless female freedom fighter."

Robyn slowly looked him up and down and smiled.

"Well, if it isn't the Sheriff of Nottingham, the pampered pompous pig."

Another wave of laughter swept over the platform.

Before the Sheriff could frame a retort, Robyn continued.

"By the way, Sheriff, I have a message for you."

"A message?" he replied, his voice suspicious.

"Yes, from Princess Phillipa." She could tell that, in spite of himself, his curiosity was aroused.

"What's the message?"

"She wants me to tell you she thinks of you at night."

A hesitant smile appeared at the corners of the Sheriff's mouth.

"Really?"

"Certainly. She says it's easier to go to sleep with nothing on her mind!"

The roar of laughter from the crowd was the loudest yet.

"Hold your tongue, gallows meat, or I'll have it torn from your throat!" roared the Sheriff.

He spun round. "Bailiff!"

The town bailiff, who had been standing at the back of

the platform, hurried forward. In his hand he carried a large scroll.

"Read the charges!"

Mindful of the drama of the moment, the bailiff, a small man, drew himself up to his full height and began to slowly unravel the scroll.

"Get on with it, man!" barked the Sheriff impatiently.

"Yes, my Lord Sheriff," came the hasty response. He fumbled nervously with the scroll, which slipped through his hands and fell to the platform.

"God's wounds!"

"Sorry, my Lord Sheriff."

As the flustered bailiff retrieved the scroll and began to unroll it, Robyn looked around her. Although she was aware her situation bordered on hopeless, the support of the crowd, the humiliation of Sir Guy and the Sheriff's discomfort had buoyed her confidence and made her more determined than ever to show her courage.

The bailiff was now holding the scroll in front of him. He cleared his throat.

"Robyn Hood, you are charged this day with the following crimes: Inciting rebellion against the lawful forces of the Lord High Sheriff."

A rumble of approval rolled through the crowd.

Striving to keep his voice clear and steady and bailiff continued.

"Giving aid and comfort to the enemies of the Lord High Sheriff."

A second rumble of approval was punctuated by cheers.

Nervously the bailiff looked at Sheriff who face showed his increasing fury.

"Get with it!" he barked.

Taking a deep breath the bailiff shouted the last charge above the increasing noise of the crowd.

"Receiving and distributing the unlawful proceeds of armed robbery!"

The applause was tumultuous.

Eyes blazing, the Sheriff swung round and glowered menacingly at Robyn.

"Robyn Hood, you're charged with treason, and crimes against the state. If this court should find you guilty your fate will be death."

Robyn remained silent, meeting his stare unflinchingly.

The Sheriff's voice rose.

"Robyn Hood, you have now heard the charges. You are permitted to speak briefly before I pass sentence upon you."

Surprised she was allowed to speak, Robyn quickly responded.

"All this time I have opposed you. I have fought against your evil deeds. All the laws you say I've broken are designed only to meet your selfish needs."

The Sheriff opened his mouth to speak, but Robyn pressed on.

"You care nothing for the people. You care only for yourself. You're a tyrant driven solely by a greed for power and a greed for wealth!"

A loud cheer from the crowd was followed by a chant of, "Robyn! Robyn! Robyn Hood!"

"Silence, outlaw! You are lying and I will listen to no more!"

The Sheriff was clearly fighting to keep his temper. After several deep breaths he turned towards the crowd and signalled to his soldiers. Their pointed lances quickly reduced the shouts of the crowd to angry murmurs.

"This court, over which I preside, has reached its verdict," began the Sheriff. "On all charges, you, Robyn Hood, are guilty!" He whirled round to face the crowd. "Guilty!" he proclaimed loudly.

His announcement was greeted with angry shouts of, "No!" and "Not guilty!"

Robyn was almost beginning to enjoy the occasion. In spite of the Sheriff's verdict, she was increasingly heartened by the support of the citizens of Nottingham.

The Sheriff smiled grimly and looked across to the captain of the guard, who was watching him from near the platform's edge. The Sheriff nodded and turned back to the crowd.

"The outlaw is guilty. Guilty! Anyone disagree?"

The captain barked an order, and several of the flanking soldiers plunged into the crowd and dragged out six citizens.

"Up here!" commanded the Sheriff.

The soldiers forced the three men and three women up the steps until they were in front of the Sheriff, then formed a menacing semi-circle around them. The men and women huddled together with downcast eyes.

The Sheriff thrust his face close to a small elderly woman's.

"Robyn Hood the outlaw is guilty. You agree, good wife?" His voice was soft with menace.

The trembling woman kept her head down and wiped her eyes and nose with the back of her sleeve.

"Um–"

"Guilty?"

"Ahh–"

The Sheriff nodded to one of the soldiers who drew a dagger, thrusting the point under the unfortunate woman's chin. Her head was forced up to meet the Sheriff's intimidating gaze.

An uneasy silence descended over the crowd as they listened intently for the woman's answer.

"Guilty?" His face was inches from hers as he hissed the question. His spittle hit the side of her face, but she made no move to wipe it off.

"Guilty." Her response was barely audible.

"Louder, citizen," he barked.

"Guilty."

"Louder!"

"Guilty!" she cried in a cracked voice before sinking to her knees and sobbing.

The Sheriff turned to the other five as the soldiers forced them into a tighter group.

"You agree, citizens?"

There was an uncertain silence. The Sheriff nodded again and the hiss of swords being withdrawn from the soldiers' scabbards sounded throughout the town square.

"Guilty? Yes?"

A ragged youth muttered "Guilty". He was echoed by two young women, one cradling a baby. A tall young man stared defiantly at the Sheriff until a sharp blow on the back of his head elicited a "Guilty" response.

The last to succumb was a bright-eyed young woman who had stood with her head held high throughout the interrogation. With a leer, the Sheriff stepped forward and put his mouth close to her ear.

"Listen carefully, my pretty. If you do not immediately shout 'guilty', I will hand you over to the captain of the guard – as a gift from me to his soldiers." He paused, and in a barely audible voice added, "To do with you as they wish."

The girl shuddered.

"As. They. Wish," repeated the Sheriff.

Her voice trembled as she forced the word out: "Guilty."

The Sheriff looked down at the uplifted faces.

"These six citizens have unanimously, and of their own free will, declared the outlaw Robyn Hood to be guilty."

He nodded to the captain of the guard, who barked an order. The phalanx of soldiers, their lances pointed at the citizens, slowly moved forward.

The Sheriff began to chant, beating time with his arms: "Guilty! Guilty! Guilty! Guilty!" The soldiers picked up the chant.

Intimidated, the citizens at the front joined in the chant. At first they mumbled, but as the advancing soldiers knocked several citizens to the ground, others joined in and the chant grew in volume. Hysteria began to flow through the throng. Caught up in the rhythm and volume, they eventually joined in: "Guilty! Guilty! Guilty!"

"Prepare the gibbet!" ordered the Sheriff.

Robyn was frightened by the crowd's change of mood. As the chant echoed through the town square, the Sheriff's triumphant smile filled her with dread. Looking around desperately, she noticed that the blue sky had begun to darken. She gazed upwards, and heard a distant roll of thunder. Then a giant flash of lightning blazed across the heavens, illuminating the Sheriff, soldiers and citizens with an unearthly glow.

As the glow faded, every person stood frozen in a giant tableau. Robyn gaped in disbelief at the uncanny scene.

A movement on the edge of the motionless crowd caught her eye. To her astonishment and joy, Robyn saw Pip at the head of the outlaw band, moving swiftly towards the platform. With mounting excitement she watched as they climbed the steps and ran towards their leader.

Robyn tried to run forward to greet them, but found she was rooted to the spot.

"Pip!" she shouted.

Although her sister was coming closer and closer, she showed no sign of recognition, and at the last moment abruptly veered away. Baffled, Robyn turned and watched her disappear into the blackness at the rear of the platform.

She spun round to see Joan coming towards her.

"Joan!"

Robyn stretched out her arms, but at the last moment her friend also swerved aside, following Pip.

One after another, Ellen, Freya, red-haired Colleen, the twins and the remaining outlaws all ran towards her, but veered away at the last moment. By the time the last one had raced past her, Robyn was in despair.

As the sky darkened further, Robyn saw another group of young women running towards her. As they came closer she saw that they were dressed in Eastlake Girls School uniforms. As they approached, each shouted an accusation at her, then, like the outlaws, veered away.

"Robyn Howard! Rude and rebellious!"

"Often late for class!"

"Always disobedient!"

"Deserves to be punished!"

"Put her in detention!"

"Yes, detention!"

By now Robyn was thoroughly frightened and bewildered by the rapid and inexplicable changes. She was on the verge of despair when she saw Willow mounting the platform and, with measured steps, making her way past the motionless Sheriff, Sir Guy and the soldiers. Hope began to return when she saw that Willow, unlike the others, was walking directly towards her. Stopping in front of Robyn, she stared unblinkingly at her. Her dark eyes had an incandescent glow that shone in the fading light.

"Robyn," she murmured softly. Her voice seemed to be coming from a distant place.

"Help me, Willow!" Robyn's voice was urgent.

Her reply, though soft, was crystal clear. "All will be well with you, Robyn."

Her eyes held Robyn's for a moment longer before she suddenly thrust her right arm skywards.

A colossal series of thunderclaps rolled across the scene, immediately followed by a giant lightning flash. Blinded, Robyn staggered back and fell heavily to the floor of the platform.

Chapter 15

Robyn stirred and slowly opened her eyes. The unfamiliar walls of the room were decorated with posters encouraging the regular brushing of teeth, and the eating of five plus fruit and vegetables a day.

"What is this place?"

"You're in the school sick bay, Robyn," replied Miss Barnes from the side of the bed. "We brought you here after the storm. The lightning and thunder caused you to fall. You were knocked unconscious."

Mrs Webster, the school nurse, leaned forward and wiped Robyn's forehead with a damp cloth. "How do you feel?" she asked.

"Fine, I think," replied Robyn, slowly sitting up.

"You lay still for a long time, then stirred and started smiling in your sleep," said Mrs Webster. "Your temperature was normal, so I thought it best to let you sleep. A few minutes before you woke, you became quite restless and started stretching out your arms. Then you calmed down, spoke a few words and began to wake up."

Robyn frowned in concentration. "What did I say?"

"*All will be well with you*," replied Miss Barnes.

Robyn stared at her and repeated slowly, "All will be well with you." She stared unseeingly at the posters as conflicting thoughts crowded her memory.

"Are you sure you're feeling better, Robyn?"

Mrs Webster's voice brought her back to reality.

"Yes, I think so."

"We rang your dad. He should be here at any moment."

"He is," said a voice from the doorway.

Robyn turned in delight, scrambled off the small bed to hug her father tightly.

"You OK, darling?" he asked.

She snuggled closer into his chest. "Yes, Dad. I feel fine."

They held each other for a long moment until Robyn looked up at him. He smiled gently.

"That's good, darling. You're still a little pale. Come on." He guided her back to the bed. "Now relax and take it easy. You gave us all a bit of a fright." He frowned briefly.

"It's all been a bit overwhelming," Robyn replied, lying down again.

"Your friends have all been phoning, asking about you."

"Have they? I must call them back."

"Yes. Oh, and a young man also rang. Said his name was William, um–"

"William Saunders." She paused. "Why did he ring?"

"He just wanted to know how you were, and–"

"And what, Dad?"

"I'm not quite sure, but I think he said something about a school ball."

"Did he?" Robyn smiled.

"Yes, he did," said a voice.

Robyn looked up to see William standing in the doorway.

"May I come in?"

"William!"

Robyn smiled warmly as William entered the room.

Her father stretched out his hand. "Hello, William. I'm Robyn's dad."

"Hello, Mr Howard," replied William as they shook hands. "I hope it's all right to come. I heard the news and thought I'd come and see how she was."

"Mrs Webster," said Miss Barnes. "Could I talk to you about something?"

The teacher started walking towards the door. Mrs Webster looked a little puzzled until Miss Barnes raised her eyebrows and nodded in the direction of Robyn and William.

"Of course, Miss Barnes."

As they left the room, Robyn's father's cell phone rang.

"Charles Howard," he said. He listened to the response and then, with a muttered, "Excuse me," he too left the room.

After a quick glance at the doorway, William sat down on the side of the bed and took Robyn's hand.

"Are you sure you're OK? It all sounded very dramatic, thunder and a lightning strike—"

"Yes, William," said Robyn. She frowned. "I had a vivid dream that I have to think through." Sensing William was about to speak, she squeezed his hand and quickly continued. "But I'm OK. Especially now."

"Now?"

"Yes, now." She hesitated. "Look, I'm sorry I was rude to you. It was just that–"

"We were both at fault. I could have been more understanding."

"Well, now you mention it–"

"Hold on," said William with a smile. "We've both admitted we could have done better. Let's just–"

"Leave it at that." Her smile was mischievous. "Is there something you wanted to ask me?"

"Yes. The school ball."

"Oh," responded Robyn innocently. "The school ball."

"You're going to make me ask again, aren't you?"

She smiled and held his gaze.

"OK." He squeezed her hand. "Would you like to come to the school ball as my partner?"

"Why, William, I thought you'd never ask." She grinned widely. "Thank you. I'd be delighted."

"So would I." He leaned forward and kissed her gently.

A discreet cough from the doorway startled them both.

"Excuse me," said Robyn's dad, smiling. "Someone wants to speak to you."

Surprised, Robyn took the phone. "Who?"

"You'll see."

"Hello?" she said uncertainly.

"Robyn, it's Mum. I'll be seeing you tonight."

"Oh my God. I thought you–"

"I was, but I've changed my plans. I'm flying home immediately."

"Oh, er … good," responded Robyn, a little doubtfully.

"Are you all right, dear? Dad said you'd had a bit of an accident."

"Yes, Mum. I'm fine."

"I'm so pleased. I got a bit of a shock when Dad rang and told me what had happened to you. We had a long talk about us."

"Us?"

"Yes. You, me and Dad."

"Oh."

"I've already made up my mind to cut back on my travels and spend more time at home."

"Are you sure, Mum?"

"Yes, darling. Your accident made me realise how precious you are to me. You're growing up fast and I've missed out on too much already. I need to spend more time with you, so I've resolved to reduce my business and travel commitments." She paused. "Now, sweetheart, about the archery tournament on Saturday – will you be OK to come with me?"

"The archery tournament?"

"Yes, dear. Like we originally planned. Will you be up to it?"

"Yes, Mum."

"It's been a while. You may be a little out of practice, darling."

Robyn smiled as a distant memory half-formed in her mind.

"Yes, Mum, but I have a strange feeling that all my arrows have a good chance of being on target."

She handed the phone back and smiled. "Dad, are you still researching the Howard family tree?"

"Yes, dear. Why?"

"I think you should have a closer look at the family outlaws that you mentioned. You may find a few surprises."

"Surprises. How do you know?"

"Not sure, Dad. I just have a strong feeling that there's much more to be discovered."

Later that night, Robyn lay in bed, her body tired but her head filled with a confusion of memories and impressions. At the same time she was conscious of a growing resolution within her. She was increasingly aware of how those in power were able to exploit groups of less fortunate people. It was unjust and unfair, and it had to be opposed.

She remembered a quote from a book on modern history that had impressed her: *The only thing necessary for the triumph of evil is that good men do nothing.*

"Or good women," she said to herself.

She turned over and snuggled deep down under her blankets, murmuring, "I'll think about it in the morning."

As she slowly drifted off to sleep, a song kept running through the back of her mind.

We're the band of Robyn Hood
We live in the forest glen.
We fight for truth and justice,
Against the Sheriff's men.

A female band of outlaws
We fight against our foes,
With sturdy shields and broadswords,
With arrows and with bows.

The Author

John Reynolds was born in Auckland, New Zealand. He is a qualified teacher, and has lived and worked in many parts of the world, including England, Saskatchewan Canada, Zimbabwe, USA and Australia.

After completing a BA in History at the University of Auckland, he completed an MA at San Jose State University (with the assistance of a Creative New Zealand grant), and a PhD at the University of Auckland on the life and works of New Zealand pioneer filmmaker John O'Shea.

As well as being a freelance author and scriptwriter, he has lectured on Media Studies and related areas at a number of tertiary institutions.

John has extensive experience in TV and radio, and public speaking. He is available to talk to schools and theatre groups about various aspects of his writing (either in person or through social media), and can be contacted directly at jbess@vodafone.co.nz, or through his website: drjohnreynolds.com.

Acknowledgements

My thanks go to a number of people who have supported me in writing this book.

I'd like to acknowledge my long-time friend and talented Auckland composer Gary Daverne, with whom I co-wrote the musical of the same name. Over the years its increasing popularity with school and theatre groups in various parts of the world encouraged me to adapt and expand the storyline into a book.

To the group of Year 10 students at Auckland's Diocesan School for Girls who undertook a "blind reading" of the first draft; thank you for your positive comments and insightful suggestions, all of which encouraged me to complete this project.

To Victoria Hunt for her talent and skill with a challenging bow.

To Natalie Hunter for her valuable assistance and encouragement.

To editors Sue Copsey and Bev Robitai, my special thanks for spotting the errors and highlighting ways in which the sentence and paragraph structure could be tightened to improve the flow.

To my friends and colleagues of the Mairangi Writers, whose critical comments have been most helpful as the book slowly took shape.

To Martin Taylor of Digital Strategies for his invaluable advice in guiding me through the various stages of publication and promotion.

To my friends and family, who have continually provided on-going support and encouragement.

Finally, my warmest thanks to Bess, my muse and my talented and loving wife, who has always supported me in whatever I have done.

By the same author

Publications

Camera in the Classroom
Media Matter
Uncommon Enemy (available as an eBook on Amazon.com)
Writing Your First Novel (available as an eBook on Amazon.com)

Musicals

Robyn Hood Outlaw Princess (Music: Gary Daverne)
Starblaze (Music: Shade Smith)
Windust (Music: Shade Smith)
Valley of the Voodons (Music: Shade Smith)

All musicals available through Stagescripts (www.stagescripts.com) or direct from the author.

The Musical

Robyn Hood Outlaw Princess is based on a musical by the same name. John Reynolds wrote the storyline and lyrics, and composer Gary Daverne wrote the music and orchestration.

The musical has been widely performed by schools and theatre groups in a number of countries, including New Zealand, Australia, Canada, the USA and England. The universal appeal of the Robin Hood legend – the strong storyline, the variety of characters, and the range of high-quality melodies have been major factors in its popularity.

For further details on the musical, including sample songs and scripts, contact Stagescripts (www.stagescripts.com), or email the authors direct: John Reynolds (jbess@vodafone.co.nz) or Gary Daverne (daverne@ihug.co.nz).